LAST BUT NOT LEASHED

A Magical Romantic Comedy (with a body count)

RJ BLAIN

ONE

There was nothing quite like starting my
week with a serious case of
petrification.

THERE WAS nothing quite like starting my week with a
serious case of petrification. What had I been thinking when
I'd applied to be a contractor for the CDC? Ever since I'd
become the Center for Disease Control and Prevention's
dog, I'd almost come to a premature end more times than I
cared to count.

Ah, right. They'd bribed me with fifty an hour, full benefits, hazard pay, paid training, and a boss I'd kill for if she
asked it of me. It was a good thing Ethel Frankwell was as
straight laced as they came, else I'd be putting my lycanthropy virus to use in all the wrong ways.

If my virus had its way, I'd be taking her home with me
and never letting her out of my bedroom ever again.

I needed a new job before I went insane, and it wouldn't
be the job hazards that finally got to me. It'd be Ethel
Frankwell, her mousy brown hair, her doe-sweet eyes, and
her hypnotizing hips. Facing my boss tested my limits on a

good day, but nothing made my day quite like watching her stomp off when someone stirred her ire.

I could handle petrification; it happened at least once a month in my line of work. Facing my boss post-petrification while I clutched a gorgon's throat with one hand and trapped a pixie with the other wasn't a good start to my Monday.

In the moments before I'd been petrified, the gorgon had been out for the pixie's blood, not that I blamed her; on a good day, I considered thinning the pixie populations in the name of world peace. Coming between them kept someone from getting killed, but I'd taken a full dose of gorgon spittle to the face. Add in her gaze, and it hadn't taken long for me to black out.

The gorgon still hissed, but a black bag over her head kept her from petrifying me again.

The pixie beat my hand with her glittery wings, her arms crossed over her chest, indulging in a pixie-typical sulk. Unfortunately for me, she didn't produce any dust.

A good hit of pixie dust would make facing my boss a lot easier.

"Earth to Dale." My boss waved her hand in front of my face. The motion wafted her perfume straight to my nose. While the other wolves in my pack found the floral scent disturbing at best, I wanted to inhale, savor the aroma, and shift to my wolf so I could rub against her legs. I didn't dare take even a sniff, as I couldn't afford her suspecting I wanted to follow her around like a puppy.

My boss waited in expectant silence, one of her eyebrows arched. As always, my tongue fought me following petrification, the first to harden, the last to soften. At least I wasn't prone to falling over while the neutralizer did its work; my sense of balance returned first, an oddity that made me an ideal employee for the CDC.

They liked sending me in to deal with cranky gorgons, and they didn't care how often I needed to gargle neutralizer to regain control over my tongue.

I really needed a new job.

As my tongue refused to obey my demands, I thrust the pixie towards my boss and hoped for the best.

"Not fair," the winged menace whined. "I only pulled one of her snakes. It's not that big of a deal."

My boss didn't look impressed, and I almost pitied the pixie. "You provoked a gorgon in a public place, resulting in the petrification of a CDC employee. It's a big deal, especially if Mr. Jameson doesn't fully recover without additional intervention." Seizing the pixie around her waist, my boss pried her out of my still-stiff hand and lifted her up. "Why did you pull on her snake?"

"She looked bored."

I'd gotten petrified because a pixie had thought a gorgon looked bored? Fifty an hour plus benefits wasn't worth it, but I couldn't force myself to quit. Unless I was willing to show off my hybrid form, a solid hell no as far as I was concerned, my prospects were few and far between.

No one trusted a lycanthrope who refused to openly shift.

My boss cleared her throat, her first warning I wasn't paying enough attention to her. With wide eyes, I gave her my full attention. "Go ahead and say whatever it is you're thinking, Dale. I'm woman enough to handle it."

I forced open my uncooperative fingers, releasing the gorgon. The stiffness in my joints would linger for hours, and I grimaced at the crack and pops in my knuckles. I swallowed and tested my tongue, pleased to discover it moved at my command. Straightening my shoulders and ignoring their creaking, I said, "Everything is fine, ma'am. I intervened when it seemed likely the ladies would engage physically. I didn't witness the triggering incident."

"Your tongue recovered faster than usual. Good. There's an ambulance out front. As soon as you can walk without falling on your face, go get checked. I'll take care of these two. If they want to send you to the hospital, have someone notify me before they haul you off."

"Yes, ma'am." Following petrification, my body wanted nothing to do with moving, and I staggered several steps before I caught my balance. Unless I shifted, I estimated it'd be several hours before the stiffness faded, but I refused.

If anyone saw my fur, they'd die of laughter while I died from embarrassment.

Every other lycanthrope I'd met had normal fur, with red and tawny counting as exotic among wolves. At my first shift, I'd been coal black, an uncommon but desirable color. A year later, everything had changed during the spring shed. My black fur had fallen out to be replaced with a wretched electric purple. Worse, not only was I electric purple, my paws, the tips of my ears, and tail were bright blue. No matter how often I checked my reflection in the mirror, I came to the same conclusion: I looked ridiculous.

Once I added in my second secret, my life was a mess. No one knew I could shift into the prized hybrid form. If I could deal with my fur color, I'd be in a much better position. I could find a different job, and often enough, human women considered hybrid lycanthropes as prospective husband material.

I had no idea what my boss was; her perfume confused

my nose on a good day and made me want to drool over her, crippling my ability to distinguish much about her by scent.

At a slow, pained walk, I headed outside to the waiting ambulance, hoping I wouldn't have to go to the hospital. If I did, I'd face another round of scrutiny regarding my elevated virus levels and rare shifts. My virus levels were consistently high enough I needed to disclose my status to employers, co-workers, and anyone who asked.

Some days, I considered wearing dog tags to make it clear I was contagious; it'd save me a lot of time and trouble.

I sighed, staggered to the ambulance, and waited for the paramedics to decide how they wanted to handle me without running the risk of becoming lycanthropes, too. Despite the fact I wasn't bleeding or even drooling, their first step was to spray me down with pink, shimmering neutralizer to eliminate any chance of them contracting my virus.

With them already nervous, I hoped they wouldn't ask about my first shift; for someone exposed before birth, I'd been abnormally old when I'd had my first shift. As far as I was concerned, my status as a late-bloomer was the closest thing to normal about me.

Resigned to a hell-filled Monday, I endured their poking and prodding, hoping to dodge an unwanted trip to a medical interrogation overseen by doctors who wanted to study me more than they cared about my health.

I DODGED A MEDICAL INTERROGATION, but when my boss offered a paid day off work to recover from petrification, my pride demanded I refuse. A double dose of neutralizer added a pink sheen and shine to my clothes, and it'd take at least five washes to get it out of my hair. In the overhead lights, my mall security jacket gleamed.

Most would recognize the signs of recent neutralizer exposure, so I didn't fret too much over my battered professionalism. For a few hours, I'd even enjoy having pale hair; as a rebellious teen, I'd tried to bleach it blond, but the incubating virus refused to cooperate. The neutralizer's nefarious tingling would drive me to the brink of insanity by the end of my shift, but I'd survive. Most lycanthropes loved the sensation, which was a little like a good scratch behind the ears and a lot like how I reacted whenever my boss got too close for my comfort.

Nervous. Wired. Interested—too interested.

At least my virus didn't act up when any woman crossed my path. A few members of the pack had that problem, and it caused nothing but trouble. Half the time, our pack's alphas, Jerome and Allison, dealt with it. The other half of the time, the problems were dumped on my lap, as I was the pack's only unmated, post-shift wolf who didn't trigger territory disputes and could, when necessary, hit hard enough to knock sense back into most of the males. Jerome thought I'd be just as good at my job within the pack if I ever got around to mating.

It wasn't my strength that kept the other wolves in line. It was me. As such, I held the dubious rank of pack beta, one of three. Among the betas, I came in dead last, as I preferred to avoid conflict rather than wade in and break up the fights before they became fights.

My father would be proud if he found out. My mother would be annoyed. She still hadn't had her first shift, and unlike me, she wouldn't have the hybrid form. My father didn't have it. My grandparents weren't lycanthropes. No one was really sure how my father had been infected.

If I hadn't been a chip off my father's block, I might've worried my mother had dallied with another lycanthrope before infection, another reason I didn't want anyone to know I had the prized hybrid form.

I should have been just like my father, with gray fur and only the wolf form. I envied my father and his perfectly normal coat. He still thought I had black fur, which was why I hadn't gone home in five years.

When my parents found out the truth, they'd laugh for a year.

The rest of my shift went by without incident—well, as without incident as a mall visited by the weirder and weirder got on a Monday. The second fight of the day broke up after a single growl from me. To cap my already shitty day, a centaur high on pixie dust just wanted a friend, and I'd been recruited as the one most likely to survive without permanent disfigurement.

The lioness scratched me four times and only tried to get into my pants once, a victory in my book, especially since she didn't mind having neutralizer foam rubbed into her fur so she wouldn't spread my virus around. Even better, she let me herd her into a cab, allowing me to get away without having to contact the CDC.

The incident would be filed in my report, I'd face a scolding from my boss for daring to shed a drop of my blood in a public place, and since nothing made sense when it came to the CDC, she'd be writing a hazard pay check while she did it.

It was only Monday, and I'd be heading home with a

week's worth of extra pay for putting up with a mall security shift.

Twenty minutes before closing, the mall's head of security tracked me down and flashed a gap-toothed grin at me. "Mr. Jameson, thank you for coming in today. Were you told about the circumstances bringing you here today?"

Before shipping me to the mall, my boss had given me an earful about the situation. A lycanthrope with a death wish had attacked one of the security guards during his last round, a round I was about to take. "Your employee was attacked after closing last night," I dutifully replied.

"Yes. It happened during the tail end of his exterior check of the building. Miss Frankwell told me you can handle a lycanthrope attack without risk of infection?"

However much I obsessed over my boss, I suspected she lived to vex me. One of the first things she did was notify my contact of my status as a lycanthrope. Why had she neglected to tell Mr. Coolridge I was beyond being infected? "I'm a lycanthrope, so yes." I tensed, waiting for his reaction.

Some didn't care about the contagion risk. Others recoiled a few feet and reeked of terror.

"Good. I was worried they'd send someone else to be infected. I'll be honest, you're the first lycanthrope I've worked with, but I like what I see so far. Are all lycanthropes able to hold up so well on long shifts?"

Then there were men like Mr. Coolridge, who realized the virus had advantages and wanted to profit from it, although more job choices for others with the virus was a good thing. "That depends on the lycanthrope, sir. If a lycanthrope has a well-developed virus, yes. Preliminary infections don't offer many benefits."

Mr. Coolridge circled me, looking me over from head to toe. "And how long have you been infected, son?"

"I was born exposed, sir. My father's a lycanthrope. I wasn't confirmed infected until I was ten. In cases like mine, the first shift can happen as early as fifteen, but it can take longer, too. I was projected to have my first shift in my forties. It typically takes several decades for the virus to develop enough to allow for shifting."

I wouldn't tell the man I'd endured a virus spike shortly after meeting my boss, something that'd resulted in me shifting fifteen years ahead of schedule. It was listed in my file that I'd had my first shift, and my fur color was still listed as pure black. Depending on if the rep with the CDC was having a bad day, I might end up with a fine for not notifying the organization my coat had changed colors. I had no idea what they'd do when they learned I had access to the hybrid form.

I suspected I'd be slapped with another fine and put to work on even more dangerous cases under a new boss.

No matter how many times I bitched and moaned about my job sucking, I didn't want a new boss. I liked the one I had, and I enjoyed not having to follow her around like a love-sick puppy to be near her.

Mr. Coolridge circled me again before he came to a halt and nodded. "Interesting. And you're contagious?"

"Yes, sir. Miss Frankwell didn't provide you with my statistics sheet?"

"I didn't bother reading it. I prefer to judge a man by his actions rather than look over what some paper shuffler sends me. She informed me you had security experience. That's all I needed to know. Have you ever infected anyone?"

"No, sir."

"Interesting."

If I'd been in my hybrid form, I would've pinned my ears back and bared my teeth. Professionalism demanded I maintain a neutral expression. Why did he think my care and caution with the uninfected was interesting? At a loss of what to say, I waited.

"Do you believe current prevention methods are effective?"

While tempted to refer him to the CDC's website for information on infection statistics, I resisted the urge. When trouble like his came calling, it was wisest to avoid adding to the problems, which would inevitably reach my boss. I made a show of thinking about his question. "I haven't infected anyone, sir. But the lycanthrope isn't the only liable individual in the equation. Others do need to be aware and take care. If you were to pick a fight with me and bloody my nose, infection is possible, and according to the law, I wouldn't be held liable. The lycanthrope is only liable if they started the fight, and such incidents are always verified by an angel."

"A good point. Be careful on your rounds, son. Give a holler if you run into trouble." Mr. Coolridge flipped me a salute and strolled off, pulling out a cell phone and placing a call.

According to my nose, the man was satisfied about something, and I wasn't certain why. Did he want lycanthrope security guards? The members of local packs would appreciate extra job opportunities. The risk of infection would make most think twice about trying their luck and picking a fight. It would also encourage those who wanted to be infected to pick fights.

Fortunately for most but unfortunately for me, those who wanted to become infected picked a fight with a lycanthrope with the hybrid form, hoping the virus would take hold and become strong enough. They'd be disappointed.

It wasn't the source of the infection that ensured access to the hybrid form. What it was, however, I wasn't certain. My father couldn't access the hybrid form. Had I been normal, I wouldn't have access to it, either.

I sighed, staring until my temporary boss turned the corner and headed deeper into the mall. If anyone learned I had the hybrid form, I'd rise to the top of the local eligible bachelor list, a status I didn't want. At the rate my persnickety virus rejected women, I'd die old and alone. I wouldn't die a virgin, at least, but I'd had my romp in the hay before I'd become contagious.

Dana had made it clear she wouldn't mind being stuck with me for life, but then she'd gone on to pick up the virus from a different wolf. Most days, I wasn't sure what to think of that, especially since she tried to have a new puppy every year.

Pack life sometimes drove me insane, especially when I ran into Dana at the pack gatherings. She loved everything about life as a mated pre-shift lycanthrope.

I remembered a few too many promises she broke when another wolf had wagged his tail, so I avoided her even more than she avoided me. I wasn't even sure why she avoided me; her mate was a twig of a man with a heart of gold, and he'd gone out of his way to tell me I didn't have anything to worry about.

I could be friends with Dana if I wanted.

My thoughts consumed me as I patrolled around the building, testing the exterior doors to make certain they were locked. Other security guards waited inside, though most of them were looking over their phones rather than paying attention to me. At most, I got a cursory glance to make certain I was a guard rather than someone hoping to slip in after hours.

As I made the circuit around the west side of the mall to the south side, I forced myself to pay closer attention; the attack yesterday had happened near one of the south entrances, a single door hidden down a concrete access ramp between two designer clothing stores. It took only a glance to understand why the attack had happened there; the lamp's light was out, leaving it a shadowy place ripe for an ambush.

If I ever had a chance to film a horror flick, I'd pick the entrance as the prime spot for a murder. A lycanthrope wanting to spread his virus around wouldn't have any troubles disabling and infecting a lone security guard.

Per my boss's instructions, I took my time investigating the spot, searching for ways a lycanthrope might get the jump on someone. It'd be easier to identify spots safe from a hunting lycanthrope, which was nowhere. A concrete half-wall divided the walkway from the parking lot, and there were plenty of ways for someone to scale the mall to the ledges dividing the ground and second floor.

Someone—something—growled behind me.

Assuming I wasn't about to be ripped apart by another lycanthrope, I needed a raise. In the worst-case scenario, I'd need to shift and fight. While having the hybrid form gave me strength and speed, I was likely the world's most pacifistic wolf.

Experience mattered, of which I had none.

Expecting the worst, I turned to face the source of the growls, coming nose to muzzle with a hybrid-form female. She bared her fangs and growled again. With a single sniff, my nose and virus identified her as an unmated female on the prowl. The sensation never failed to bother me.

Unmated females always gave my virus certain ideas, but my picky-as-hell virus wanted my boss, and I had no doubts the damned thing wouldn't quit until it got its way.

At least she wasn't a mated female. Whenever I got too close to a mated female, I wanted to back away at least ten feet, tense and wary the male would show up and pull out my fur for getting too close.

With a little luck, she wouldn't clue in I was a lycanthrope without a mate. If I got lucky, I'd be able to talk her down without someone—me—getting hurt.

"The mall's closed, ma'am." I relaxed so I wouldn't look like a threat, looking her over. A second sniff warned me if she didn't find a male soon, she'd act on her serious case of grumpy. She growled again, her eyes narrowing to slits.

Unmated females on the prowl had a tendency to beat on unmated males to prove they were strong enough to bear puppies.

I didn't want anyone beating on me, not even my boss. As always, my virus had different thoughts about *that*.

I needed to stop lying to myself. If my boss wanted to beat on me, I'd encourage her, run to piss her off, and push to see how far she'd go to prove her interest in me.

I stood my ground, and she lowered her head to look me in the eyes, pricking her ears forward. "Where? Not here. Where? We meet here. You not him."

Her harsh, raspy voice startled me. It had taken me several long nights of practice, but it hadn't taken me long to master English while in my hybrid form. The possibility of her being new to the third form worried me even more than the anger and annoyance rich in her scent.

The lycanthrope attack made a lot more sense when I added an unmated hybrid female into the equation.

"Are you courting one of the security guards here?"

She bobbed her head.

Sometimes, I hated when I was right. Being right almost always caused me more trouble than I wanted. If she was courting the security guard who'd been attacked, it was entirely possible someone the female knew had been involved. That the guard survived suggested the attacking wolf approved of her interest and wanted to ensure she mated.

The instant her virus detected the virus in the man she courted, she'd go into a frenzy to claim him.

He'd be one lucky man, although I didn't envy him the bites and scratches she'd inflict on him during their first mating, which would likely result in a child nine months down the road.

Frenzied females were not to be underestimated under any circumstance.

There was nothing in the CDC contractor's handbook about what to do in the case of cranky lycanthrope female seeking her desired man. I doubted the mall security guide had anything of use in it, either.

She leaned towards me, breathing in my scent. "Where is he? You wolf, too. Why here?"

Some questions I could answer, and the CDC made it easy to direct her attention away from me. "I'm a stand in hired by the CDC, ma'am. If you'll call the CDC's office here, they'll be able to give you more infor—"

The female lunged for me, slashing at my chest with her six-inch claws. I sidestepped, grabbed the wall, and jumped on top.

A pack of wolves waited on the other side, and they growled.

A cranky hybrid female viewing me as a threat to her man would cause me problems, but a small pack was more than I could handle. They were ready and itching for a fight, and I wanted to find somewhere nice and quiet to hide until they went away.

Running only stirred predatory instincts, so I stood my ground and waited.

"Where is he?" the female snarled.

"A lycanthrope attacked him. He's in the hospital. I don't know if he's infected, but it's probable. He was seriously injured. That's all I know."

The acrid bite of fury stung my nose. I doubted any of them were responsible. I held up my hands and hoped they wouldn't view me as a threat. "I'm just a CDC contractor covering for him until he recovers."

The female's ears turned back. "Where?"

"I really don't know, ma'am. The CDC does, and once you explain you're courting him, they'll give you the information you need. I just show up where and when I'm told."

Her pack drew closer, and they snarled. If I shifted to my wolf form, I might have a chance of outrunning them, as long as I was on the move before they realized I'd given them the slip. The female hopped onto the wall with me, sniffing. "You not mated. Courting?"

Why couldn't the lycanthropy virus allow for some privacy? "No and no. I'm not interested."

"Pre-shift?" She flicked an ear back. "Virus smell strong."

"There isn't anyone I'm interested in."

She huffed and her other ear turned back. "You lie. Why?"

Scowling, I lowered me hands. "Why would you say that?"

"You interested in someone. Today. Scent lingers."

If any of the pack came around after my morning meetings with my boss, I'd need to remember they might scent my interest in her on me. Why did Ethel Frankwell have to be everything I wanted in a woman?

She made hiding my interest difficult.

The truth never steered me wrong, and I wielded it as a shield. "She's unavailable."

"Your virus disagree. I smell. She wolf? Infected?"

"I don't know." If my boss was infected, her perfume hid the scent markers. Infected or not, I didn't care. It didn't matter. Mating ensured infection. No matter what, I couldn't afford to think of my boss as a potential mate.

My virus liked the idea, I liked the idea, and if I lost control, my boss would be the target of my interest.

Courting males could snap just like courting females, and when it happened, it got ugly. No, I wouldn't be one of those wolves.

I'd be more than completely certain of my future mate's interest. I'd be so certain I wouldn't make the first move, and the only way I'd settle down with a female was if she hunted me, caught me, beat me within an inch of my life, and leashed me so thoroughly I couldn't escape her even if I tried.

She shook out her fur, canted her head, and watched me. "He belong to us. CDC trade you for him, yes?"

"He's not a hostage, ma'am. He's in the hospital."

"He not here."

Why did I end up with the crazy jobs? "He's not here

because he's in the hospital. There's no need for any sort of trade. He's really not a hostage."

"You come. They talk. When they talk, you return safe. He mine. He pack," the female growled. "No run. You run, you hurt."

While I tended to be pacifistic in nature, especially for a lycanthrope, if she thought I was going to sit and accept being taken as the hostage of another pack, she was insane. "Why don't I—"

She jumped for me, taking another swipe with her claws, which tore into my upper arm. With a yelp, I recoiled, hopping back along the dividing wall so I wouldn't fall among the gathered wolves.

The scent of my blood goaded the other lycanthropes, who dove into the fray with yips and howls. While I'd gotten in some practice mock fighting with my pack, I only managed to dodge the pack's first few bites before their sharp teeth dug deep into the calf of my left leg and the wolves hauled me off the wall, slamming me into the asphalt.

Provoking a lycanthrope involved two parts: pissing off the human half and waking the virus.

My human half wanted nothing to do with bleeding, and my virus reacted just like expected: it wanted to match drop for drop and add interest. However much I disliked shifting without a good reason, my virus boiled in my veins and was tired of my shit.

It wouldn't let me go down without a fight.

When magic came out to play, physics and the laws of conservation of matter went right out the window. Many had tried to learn why a hundred and sixty pound man like me could explode from his clothes, gain an extra six hundred pounds, sprout fur, and develop an unfortunate tendency to howl at the moon in the time it took me to draw a single breath.

I called for my pack, although I held no real hope they'd hear me. I didn't spend enough time as a wolf to form the bonds the others shared. Twisting around, I smashed my paw into the wolf mauling my leg, scruffed him, and tore him off. Showing my fangs, I bellowed in the wolf's face before chucking him across the parking lot.

He crashed onto the hood and windshield of a car, its alarm singing a shrill song.

The female barked a warning. "Hybrid! You? *You?*"

I understood her astonishment completely, but before I had a chance to reply, she lunged for me. My virus's fury over being attacked and outnumbered gave me the strength to toss two more of the wolves before I fell beneath them. The female did most of the work, pinning me with her weight and sinking her claws deep into the back of my neck. "Sur-ren-der or die. Your choice."

The sharp stab of her claws burying in my throat fell under the heat of my fury, and when I tensed, she dug in deeper. The stench of my blood deadened my nose to all other scents, and while I growled, I kept still.

"Good. You stay. Pack need male hybrid. You help. You have strong virus. You share. Pack grow strong. You bring my future mate back. All be good."

I bared my teeth in defiance, and she tightened her grip, cutting off my breath.

Why, why, why did I always attract the crazy ones? Ah, right. I worked as a CDC contractor. It was in my job description. When my boss got her hands on me, she'd make the pack's attack pale in comparison.

My virus would like it, too.

"You mine now. Me stronger."

I struggled to suck in a breath, and my vision blurred. It didn't take long or my body to go limp beneath hers. When she eased her hold on me enough I could breathe, I wheezed.

"Pat. Shift. Get car. We take hybrid."

"Excuse me? You'll do what?" The amused disbelief in my boss's voice jolted me to full awareness, and I tensed. A flashlight shined in my eyes, and I growled, unable to turn to avoid the blinding beam. "This is how this is going to work. You're going to stand down, back off, and behave, or I'm going to pump so many rounds into you they'll be pulling bullets out of your hide for a week. This puppy's an M14, and if I pull the trigger, you might not even make it to the hospital. Your choice."

"Cheat," the female snarled.

"One would say nine against one is cheating, too. She who holds the M14 makes the rules, and my rules say you're the one cheating. Call your pack off, or I'm going to unleash my gun *and* the pack of angry wolves itching for a chance to beat on you for a while. It takes a lot of balls to attack one of the Baltimore pack's betas. Unless you want to die young, I recommend you back off."

The female tightened her grip on me, digging her claws deeper into my throat, spilling more of my blood. "Hybrid beta? Not alpha?"

"I'm the alpha," Jerome announced, and he redirected the flashlight out of my eyes. "The missus apologizes she can't wipe the concrete with you herself, but she's stuck at work. As for Dale, he's my beta because that's what he does best. I recommend you listen to the lady here. She really will pull the trigger. Frankly, I'm surprised she hasn't yet."

"I won't if she lets Dale go," my boss grumbled.

According to her tone, my boss wanted nothing more in life than to turn the hybrid female into paste with her fully automatic military rifle.

"Dale's going to be fine, Ethel. Sure, they've bloodied him up pretty badly; this whole lot is going to need detoxed, but he'll be fine. Just be careful, his virus is probably spiked to hell, and I make zero promises I can control him after she releases him."

"We'll play it by ear." My boss grunted. "Well, lady? What's it going to be? You going to let him go?"

"You CDC."

"Yes, I am, and you're digging your claws into *my* wolf."

"You steal my male. This male mine until my male returned."

While the crazed hybrid female allowed me to breathe, she kept her claws lodged in my throat. If my boss opened fire, I might emerge with my head still attached—maybe.

I bet I could make a fortune with a circus. Working for a circus, I wouldn't have to worry about anything other than keeping my fur pretty and showing off my inhuman strength. I'd probably even make more money, as long as I didn't mind the entire world knowing I was a freak.

"Wait, what?" my boss blurted.

"My future mate gone. You take. He work here. This male do mine's rounds. He said CDC take. You take."

"Is your future mate's name Mr. Jones?"

"My male," the female snapped.

"Mr. Jones is in the hospital undergoing treatments right now. We didn't take him. He's being given medical care."

"My pack no hurt future mate. I introduce him to pack tonight, but he not here. This male here instead! Want my male."

"Can you confirm his name?"

"San…" The female snapped her teeth. "Hard like this. My male."

I liked that the two talked; talking meant I had a substantially higher chance of escaping with only a few holes in my neck, which my virus would heal given a few hours. With Jerome nearby, if the CDC decided I'd bled too much, they'd pump me full of his blood to jumpstart my virus, which would multiply in response to his virus. As he was pack, the viruses would ultimately work together until Jerome's died out in several days.

The CDC didn't like doing it because until Jerome's virus was out of my system, I'd be prone to flying off the handle.

My boss replied, "Take your time and try again."

"San-tee-ah-go. Jones. Mine."

"If you can control yourself and your pack, I can arrange for you to see Mr. Jones," my boss offered. "After, you'll need to go to the station to answer some questions. You'll need someone to accompany you from the CDC. Mr. Jones is very sick right now, and you will be drugged if you cause trouble. You'll need to shift to your human form. The same applies to your pack."

"You no lie?"

"I make no promises you won't be fined for attacking a CDC employee, but the CDC does take circumstances into consideration. You'll have exactly one chance to cooperate before my rifle does the talking."

"Okay. Trade your male for my male."

Jerome coughed before whispering, "If you have to shoot her, she might hurt Dale even more."

"I won't have to shoot her if she cooperates."

The female released me and hopped away. "Who hurt my male? Tear apart. Yes. You let me tear apart. This be good."

The promise of violence got a chuckle out of my boss. "We're not sure who attacked Mr. Jones yet, but if we find out who, we might even let you have the first crack at him. Now, please shift." Once the female obeyed, standing naked in the parking lot, my boss barked, "Hose the lot down."

Neutralizer wouldn't reverse an infection, but it did kill the virus when outside of the body. Pale, shimmering foam rained down, and the yips of excited lycanthropes filled the air. I itched where the neutralizer got into my open wounds.

There were a lot of them.

"If she takes as much as a single step towards Dale, shoot her," my boss ordered. Footsteps drew close, and a few moments later, she crouched beside me. "All right, Dale. I need you to keep still and quiet while your virus works its magic. If you can shift to your standard wolf form, you should. You've been mauled."

I bared my fangs at her and growled to display my opinion on her request.

She swatted my snout. "No. You're going to do as you're told without snapping at me."

One little nip wouldn't hurt, would it? A single drop of my blood could spread my virus to her, a subtle claim on her no one could reverse.

If my virus could speak, it would've been singing, *Mine, mine, mine*.

The click of a safety disengaging alarmed me into rising to all fours, snarling as I searched for the source of the sound. Several cops pointed their weapons at me, waiting in tense silence. I stood and straightened to my full height, restraining the urge to shake.

I didn't want to infect them, but if they came near my boss while armed, I'd rip them apart.

"Easy, Dale. You're soaked in blood. It needs to be neutralized." My boss patted my arm. "Officers, he's not the issue. The pack attacked him. He's a CDC employee—one of my contractors. Jerome, please introduce your pack to the police while I take care of Dale."

"You got it, Ethel."

Since standing hurt, I crouched at my boss's feet, snarling and snapping my teeth whenever anyone thought about closing closer. When growling tired me, I kept my teeth visible in silent warning.

I meant to stay on guard for as long as needed, but my virus flew the white flag of surrender. Without it sustaining me, I sank into a semi-conscious daze, aware of only the presence of the woman I had no business desiring but needed anyway.

Pink and sparkly beat electric purple and blue any day of the week.

JEROME PRODDED me with his shoe, and I landed a bite on his sneaker. I spit out a chunk of leather and flattened my ears.

"You need to shift, Dale. There's no way we're going to drag your fat ass around. You're caked in neutralizer, too."

My boss snickered. "You're rather pink and sparkly right now. It's a good look on you."

Pink and sparkly beat electric purple and blue any day of the week. With a tired groan, I lurched to all fours, braced, and shook out my fur. "I don't need to be dragged, thank you. I can walk."

"You'll pass out in my truck on the way home. Your virus is tapped. Shift to your wolf so we can carry you once you go down. You're coming to my place until we're sure you won't snap like that crazed bitch and do something you regret. Don't worry about her, though, she'll be all right; she's so hopped up on pixie dust right now she won't be a threat to anyone other than herself. I thought you'd appreciate knowing. Unless you press charges, she'll get off light." Jerome prodded me again. "Once your virus recovers, you'll need to be questioned."

Talking helped me ignore the sensation of my skin tightening and itching as my virus worked to heal my battered body. "There's not much to tell. I did my rounds. The hybrid female approached me. She wanted to know where the male she's courting was. I told her to contact the CDC. She decided she needed collateral. When I said no, things got violent."

"Well, you put up a fight, I'll give you that much. You tossed a young one into a car so hard you about killed him. He'll probably survive. If he doesn't, well, no loss there. Only an idiot attacks a pack wolf and expects an easy win. You got a better look at them than we did, I suspect. Do you believe any of them attacked the bitch's male?"

I grunted and barely avoided shaking my head and tearing open the wounds on my throat again. "I don't know."

"Shift to your wolf form, Dale," my boss ordered. "We need to see how well you're healing."

With no way to escape exposing my humiliating fur color, I sighed, crouched so I wouldn't fall over during the shift, and obeyed. It took longer than I liked, more evidence my virus was nearly tapped out trying to keep me alive. I flopped onto the asphalt with a pained groan.

"Fuck. He's still bleeding." With no fear of contamination, my boss ran her fingers through my fur around my throat. "Check his leg."

Jerome batted my boss's hand aside and grabbed me by the scruff with one hand, pinning me with his weight while he leaned over me to check my hind leg. "It's still bleeding, too. I'll call in a few members of the pack. Hopefully, Allison and I can provide enough blood, but I'd feel better having the others on hand if something goes wrong. Where should we take him?"

"Nowhere; too high of a risk of spreading the virus. We'll do the transfusion here, wait for the wounds to close, and hose the lot down again. It's your lucky day, Dale. You're about to get a hit of the best pixie dust money can buy, and I get to be the one holding your leash. It'll be a literal leash, too. We're going to have a great time."

"But I was going to take him home with me," Jerome protested.

"Not while he's under the influence of pixie dust you're not. He's going home with me."

My flagging virus liked any attention she gave me, but I worried. When my boss sounded so pleased and eager to defy Jerome, she was causing trouble for someone. Me. The kind of trouble I wanted wasn't up on offer, but as I had no real say in the matter, I surrendered without a fight and hoped for the best.

Sometimes, I was an idiot like that.

MY PACK LAUGHED AT ME, and I couldn't blame them for their mirth. In the bright spotlight illuminating the parking lot, there was no way for me to hide the color of my fur. Jerome's mate, Allison, laughed the hardest. "This explains so much. Most of us would kill to have the hybrid form, but I can totally understand your hesitancy with that fur color. How long have you had access to the hybrid form, Dale?"

I refused to meet her gaze, turning my head to discover

my ex-girlfriend, her mate, Pete, and all six of their puppies staring at me intently.

"Yes, do tell, Dale," my ex said. "Just how long have you been a hybrid?"

Thanks to the transfusion, which fed Jerome's blood into my right forepaw, I couldn't run away and hide, which was my preferred method of dealing with uncomfortable questions. The other way, a silent, reproachful glare, had lost its effectiveness.

"Don't be so shy," she muttered. "Are you seriously telling me one of your parents is a hybrid?"

My boss placed her hand on the top of my head, pressing down with enough force I froze, uncertain what had stirred her ire. "Neither of Dale's parents are hybrids. Until now, the source of his father's infection was unknown." When Dana didn't reply, my boss lifted her hand and turned her attention to the line feeding me a bag of blood stolen from Jerome. "I've heard of lycanthropes with this color strain, and they all come from the same place. It's more unusual that Dale's father isn't the same color."

My boss knew how my father had contracted the lycanthropy virus? I lifted my head and pricked my ears.

"A hot spot near Ocean City," she explained. "It had a one percent infection rate and flared for a single day before burning out. Your father puts the known count of infected up to nine individuals, assuming we can confirm the strain through a blood test. You might just be an oddity."

I flatted my ears and whined.

She rolled her eyes. "A handsome oddity. Does that make you feel better? Come on, Dale. I never pegged you as the type to have self-esteem issues. You're usually so confident and comfortable with yourself."

While it pleased me I'd managed to fool her, I worried she'd be disappointed in the truth. Me? Confident? I couldn't even shift to my wolf without wanting to hide.

"You think he's handsome?" my ex blurted.

I flinched at the astonishment in Dana's voice, but I didn't quite dare to growl, not with Pete and her puppies nearby.

"Darlin', if you weren't aware he could leave a trail of dropped panties and panting ladies in his wake, you haven't been paying attention." My boss huffed, shook her head, and checked the bag. "Next bag, Jerome. Still your blood?"

"There's one of mine left. Allison has three of hers waiting in the cooler. If that doesn't jumpstart his virus, he's going to need at least a week of peace and quiet to recover."

"Meter," my boss ordered.

I growled and attempted to tuck my paws under me so I wouldn't be subjected to yet another poke. Jerome joined forces with my boss, holding me by the scruff so she could stab me and check my virus levels.

"Still low, but not dangerously so," she reported. "Do the rest of the bags while I call the neutralizer tanker back so we can hose the place down again. Allison, think you can run the rest of the bags into him at one time so we aren't here all night?"

Jerome's mate snickered. "He has four paws, so I don't see why not. He's going to be so hopped up on the virus you really will need to dose him with pixie dust to control him once we're done."

"I'm calling in for the dust along with the tanker. If I have to dose him, he really is coming home with me since I'm the only idiot in the area with the right training to handle someone under the influence of the highest grades of pixie dust. Try not to let him give you the slip while I'm gone. There's been enough excitement for one day."

INFECTING AN ALREADY INFECTED lycanthrope with high concentrations of the virus usually led to trouble, a blood bath, or both. Sometime between stabbed with a meter and stuffed full of virus-contaminated blood, my boss lived up to her threat of dosing me with the type of pixie dust the CDC kept under lock and key.

Within minutes of the injection, I went from snarling my discontent to trying to purr. Purring wasn't one of my skillsets, and it emerged more as a rumbly growl, but I tried anyway.

Why couldn't wolves purr? I wanted to purr.

At my boss's order, someone hosed me down with neutralizer, and I rolled in the foam, wagging my tail and kicking my paws at the way it made my skin tingle.

"Dale, please come here," she ordered.

As neither my virus nor I saw any need to disobey and rather enjoyed being closer to her, I surged to my paws, bounded over, and leaned against her legs. She sighed, which I took as an invitation to flop over onto her feet and show her my belly.

"Are you really sure you want to handle him alone, Ethel?" Jerome knelt beside me and scratched under my chin. I melted under his affection, and he laughed. "Pixie dust is great. I never would've guessed Dale enjoys attention. That'll make it easier down the road, assuming we can convince him to wear his fur coat more often."

"I'll have a talk with him about it," my boss promised.

"Are any of your pack fighters free tomorrow? I'm going to need a lycanthrope to cover his shift, and I've already booked the rest of my contractors. I'm not going to put someone who can be infected on this shift, not when there's been two attacks in as many days."

"Standard comp?"

"Double plus hazard pay; with two confirmed attacks, I can classify it as high risk. I can authorize two on the shift if two of your pack are available."

"Allison? Think you can take off work tomorrow?"

"You betcha. I'd love to get my claws on the asshole who started this mess. No one fucks with our beta and gets away with it." Allison paused. "Except for you, Ethel. You can fuck with him as much as you want. I bet he'd like it."

"Allison!" my ex squealed.

"Give me a break, Dana. Ethel's the only one Dale even looks at, and he's too damned professional to make any moves on her because she's his boss. It ain't anyone's fault other than your own that you let him go. You have an entire litter of puppies and a good mate now, and it's not like it matters that you sampled the wares. No one cares, really. Do you care, Ethel?"

I sure as hell cared they were talking about me like I was a prized specimen worthy of being passed around.

Wait. What? The idea they were even interested in gossiping about me like I was a stud worth passing around stopped me dead in my tracks, especially as the conversation involved the one woman my virus desired. It didn't help—or hurt—that I wanted her, too.

My boss chuckled. "Not at all. I'm only concerned about actual competition."

She was *what*? I blinked, my mouth dropping open,

wondering if I'd heard her correctly. Jerome scratched me behind an ear, and I slumped to the asphalt with a happy groan.

"Ladies, if you're going to discuss his prowess, I recommend you do so when Dale's coherent enough to enjoy it. The man could use a little stroking of his ego."

Allison leered, directing most of it at my boss. "Of his ego, huh?"

"Not helping," Jerome muttered.

"Sure I am. I'm making it perfectly clear Ethel shouldn't be stroking just his ego. She can stroke his ego all she wants, as far as I'm concerned. I just thought I'd impress upon them both they have our approval. Wasn't that nice of me? I'm being nice. You're always telling me I should be nicer to people. I was just doing as you wanted."

Jerome got to his feet, caught his mate in a headlock, and dragged her away. "Do whatever you want with him, Ethel. Don't listen to this menace. Just return my beta in reasonable physical and emotional health when you're finished with him."

"Reporting time for tomorrow's shift is ten. Make sure your fighters aren't late."

"Allison and I will stand in, and I promise you, we won't be late. We'll see you in the morning."

My boss patted my shoulder. "Come on, Dale. Let's get out of here before someone else decides to aim their perverted commentary in our direction."

THREE

Pixie dust was the best.

WHEN MY BOSS ordered me to relax, I obeyed in the best way possible. I took a nap in her car, surrounded by her scent. Some commands were worth following, and I would've done as she said without hesitation, even without the pixie dust.

Jerome was probably right, though. Pixie dust was the best.

Pixie dust won me an invitation into my boss's bed, and in the privacy of her home, her perfume couldn't hide the truth. She was infected with lycanthropy, too. When I thought about it, all the signs had been there from the start. She had no fear of me or any other lycanthrope. There was nothing for her to fear.

The only thing she needed to worry about was picking a mate, and as a rare unmated infected female, *she* decided which male won her. Once word spread she was unmated, every single lycanthrope in the area would be after her.

Looks didn't matter to a lycanthrope, either, although I found her more attractive than most.

My virus probably had something to do with that.

If anyone found out she was an unmated lycanthrope, I wouldn't be able to compete, not against so many other wolves. Even if I could, she was my *boss*. Wait. If I quit, just like I wanted, she wouldn't be my boss, which meant I could compete for her. Defective fur coloration aside, I did have access to the hybrid form. Mated to me long enough, her virus would develop to allow her to access the hybrid form, too. If the hybrid form enticed her, I'd sacrifice my dignity and prance around in my electric purple and blue coat for however long she wanted.

That led me back to quitting. I needed to quit first and prance second. If she didn't drive me off, shoot me, or otherwise reject my displays of interest, I'd figure something out. Ditching my job so I could attempt to convince my boss she wanted me around permanently hadn't been a serious option before.

Then she'd talked about panties being dropped in my wake. While I had no interest in the panties of other women, my virus was more than interested in discovering what sort of panties she wore, if she'd drop them for me, and if she'd accept my posturing.

Allison had spoken the truth, and I wanted to know what my boss thought about it. Ethel Frankwell was the only woman I ever looked at twice. She also snored.

I'd heard softer trains.

Learning to sleep next to the equivalent of an ongoing explosion hadn't been a part of my plans, but I'd make do. It occurred to me her snoring had woken me. Yawning, I lifted my head for a better look around. A dim glow from the hallway illuminated most of the room, which was a disaster of dirty laundry. If she cared I could see her lingerie, I'd be in trouble when she woke up. From corner to corner, lacy bras and panties waited to be cleaned up and run through the wash, which I determined was the primary source of her scent marker.

I doubted her lingerie did a good job of covering her.

Under no circumstances would I peek under the blanket to discover what she wore to bed. To keep a firm leash on myself and my virus, I wiggled off the bed, stretching out my forepaws so I wouldn't thump to the floor.

She kept snoring.

I shifted to my hybrid form and prowled around her home, inhaling in her scent and memorizing her lycanthropy marker. To my astonishment, she lived in a tiny trailer. My apartment wasn't much better, something I'd need to change if I somehow lured my boss into accepting me as her mate. While her trailer was small, rather battered, and old enough to tempt me into breaking things to give her a good excuse to move in with me, she had a washer and dryer tucked into a nook in the hallway.

Restless energy coursed through me, and the simple but tedious task of doing laundry would give me a chance to relax and regain control over my virus, which wanted me to return to bed with my boss, wake her, and test the waters to see if she was interested in me as a prospective mate.

Doing her laundry wouldn't land me in too much hot water, would it? It was challenging to tiptoe when I weighed in at eight hundred pounds, but I managed, stealthily picking my way through her room and retrieving every piece of clothing I could get my paws on, careful to avoid tearing anything with my claws.

The nightstand clock informed me it was eight in the morning, which would trigger panic in my boss when she realized she'd slept in. Then again, I'd been convinced my boss never slept; no matter how early I showed up at the office, she was always there before me.

Stealing her clothes, I sorted them, taking my time checking labels so I wouldn't ruin anything before starting the first load. Leaving the machine to work its magic on her laundry, I searched her trailer for my phone, wallet, and keys without success.

A sane man might have worried in my situation, but the thought of being at her mercy had me wagging my tail while I finished sorting through her clothes and preparing her delicates to be taken in for dry cleaning.

The shrill blare of an alarm startled me into yipping, and my boss snarled curses. The alarm fell silent. "Dale?"

I peeked into her bedroom to discover she held the mangled wreckage of her alarm in her hand. When I'd grown up and left home, my mother had never given me any helpful advice on how to handle a cranky woman in the morning.

I either needed a manual for women or a tour guide. Maybe I'd ask Jerome; he somehow survived mornings with Allison.

"My clothes are missing. Why? Where have my clothes gone?" She pointed at the cleaned floor, which was devoid of any lingerie.

"It's not missing. It's being sorted and cleaned." I displayed my long, curved claws. "These tear clothes if I walk on them, so I picked them off the floor."

"You're doing my laundry?"

I relaxed at the astonishment in her voice. "I put aside the clothes that needs to go to the dry cleaners, and I sorted the rest by material and color." Flicking an ear back, I glanced in the direction of her tiny kitchen. "I should've made coffee."

"But you're a guest. You should be in bed resting."

The 'in bed' part interested my virus, but I rejected the concept that I should lounge around because I was within her territory. For a rare change, my uppity virus agreed with me.

My role was to provide. Hers was to decide, after I made my displays of interest, if she wanted me to be her mate. Until I could provide for her in a better environment, I wouldn't be satisfied.

She deserved better.

Before I committed to taking the next step and displaying my interest, I had a few questions, although one was more important than the others. Prowling closer, I inhaled to catch her scent. "Your perfume hides the scent of your virus. Why do you hide your virus?"

"It's made from wolfsbane blossoms. Most lycanthropes hate the smell. I'm used to it. I've been helping the CDC with an experiment. The goal is to help unmated lycanthropes avoid unwanted attention by masking the scent markers. We discovered an unexpected benefit, as the perfume also helps lower virus levels. They're looking into developing it as a method to help lycanthropes stabilize their moods, especially during dangerous virus spikes. If we're lucky, it'll also help make it easier for younger lycanthropes to learn how to control their virus and their new instincts and impulses. You're one of the few lycanthropes who seems to be attracted to the scent. This is especially unusual as you have a general aversion to most women. The CDC has asked several times if I could recruit you for experiments."

The last thing I wanted was the CDC experimenting on

me. I also didn't want the organization experimenting on her, either, and my hackles rose at the thought. "There are circumstances," I growled, giving my fangs a lick.

"I'm guessing it's because I'm your boss." She laughed and sat up, her blanket falling away to reveal a silky blouse that clung to her chest, which I recognized as one of her work shirts. "It's not an issue. The CDC accounts for courting and mated pairs. I'd either remain your boss, depending on how our work dynamic changed, or you'd be elevated in rank and work alongside me as an equal. We might be moved to different departments. Some pairs work better together than others, but I expect we'd continue to work as a partnership. We've been working together long enough the CDC would hesitate to separate us. Assuming my position as your boss isn't a factor, which it is not, what would you do, Mr. Jameson?"

I liked the way she growled my name. Crouching, I fought my desire to pounce and show her in intimate detail. "What do you want me to do?"

She chuckled, a low, throaty sound. "Before I answer that, has the pixie dust worn off yet?"

Unlike alcohol, when I got hold of a dose of pixie dust, I rarely comprehended when I was under its influence. I shrugged.

"Shift to human," she ordered.

If I shifted back to human, I'd give her a full display, as I hadn't found any of my clothes in her trailer. "But I have no clothes."

Both of her brows shot up. "I gave you a full hit of the highest grade of pixie dust available. You really burned it off already?"

"I suppose."

"I prefer you when you aren't a mindless slave, so good. I've tested your patience—and your virus—for the past six years, ten months, and twenty days. After I get done with my mandatory work for the day, I'm going to call in, make sure everyone is prepared to take care of themselves for once, and make time so we can talk. Most of the talking, if I have my way, will be done in bed. Once we're done talking, we're going to discuss how we're going to track down the lycanthrope that attacked Mr. Jones."

Since when did *I* help with investigations? My boss did often enough, something that never failed to make me nervous, but I always filled in for the people unable to do their work because of the CDC—or because they were a victim and the CDC stepped in to provide help. "We are?"

"We are. After you went to bed last night, my boss called me. He thinks you're the sort of man this lycanthrope wants in his pack. You have a very similar build and appearance to Mr. Jones. Once word spreads you're an exotic hybrid, he thinks you'll be targeted. I agree with him." She smiled, and a glint in her eyes warned me of trouble brewing on the horizon. "Once word spreads I'm claiming you, you'll be irresistible."

My fur stood up on end, and I was torn between making a run for it to see if she would chase me, setting aside my need to prove I could be a suitable partner and accepting her offer without question, and testing to see if I could hide under her bed. "You want to claim me?"

"Is that truly so hard to believe?"

"Yes." I flattened my ears and tried to relax, but tension quivered through me. "I thought I'd have to quit. Then I wasn't sure what I was going to do. Beg, maybe. Being honest, I hadn't gotten far into the quitting idea."

"Well, you don't need to quit. While I suspected you might be interested, I wasn't going to push you. You're very shy, especially around women. I didn't want to scare you off."

Shaking out my fur helped me to relax despite my conflicted instincts. "I didn't want to do anything inappropriate."

"Trying to stake a claim in public is inappropriate. Staking a claim in private is encouraged and expected. No one cares as long as you maintain your professionalism. As I've never seen you be anything other than a cool professional, I don't anticipate any problems on that front. You don't have to worry."

"I hadn't gotten around to quitting because I wasn't sure what other work I could do. It was an issue."

She chuckled. "Once again, not an issue. It's really not. Now that the CDC is aware you have the hybrid form, I expect you'll be evaluated and offered training within law enforcement or a higher position in the CDC. You'll need a lot of training, though. I watched the security footage while you were having the transfusion. While you did a fine job tossing three of those wolves, the rest of your performance was awful. If I hadn't heard you speak so clearly, I would've believed it was your first round in your hybrid form."

She was kinder about my deficiencies than usual, but I still lowered my head and whined.

"Dale. There's no reason to be ashamed of your fur. You do need to learn how to protect yourself in all your forms. That's non-negotiable."

"I'm bright purple."

"And? I like it." My boss patted her bed in invitation. "Come into bed, stretch out, and relax while I take care of my morning rounds. While I expect it'll take you a long time to accept the truth, I'll show you how much I like your fur every day if necessary."

Intrigued by her offer and wondering how she intended to show me how much she liked my fur, I joined her in bed. She scratched under my chin, and I flopped onto the mattress, stretching my neck so my muzzle rested on her pillow. I meant to only close my eyes for a few moments, but her fingers in my fur and my contented virus eased me to sleep.

JEROME'S SNICKERS WOKE ME, and I growled over his interruption of my nap. "He's just catching up on sleep, Ethel. Between the strain to his virus and having a sense of security, it's no surprise he's taking advantage of the chance to rest." Someone poked my shoulder, and I growled again. "Dale, the average toddler fights better than you do, so stop snarling at me. Allison's in the kitchen making you breakfast. Up, up. You're worrying Ethel."

"He slept through yesterday and the entire night," my boss complained.

Jerome grabbed my ear and twisted. Yowling, I batted at my alpha, earning a swat across my muzzle. "Up, Dale. You're worrying Ethel, and when Ethel worries, she finds some way to annoy me. I have been annoyed enough for one week."

"Jerome." I bared my teeth and cracked open an eye. My threat of violence didn't stop him from yanking on my ear again. "I'm awake, damn it."

"See? Just get rough with him next time. A sharp tug on the ear usually does the trick. Dale, I went to your apartment and brought over some clothes for you. This trailer's a bit small for you like that, so shift already. How the hell did you get any sleep, Ethel? He's all but taken over your bed."

"I improvised. For the record, he has a very thick fur coat and is a quiet sleeper. I don't think he even noticed my weight."

"With his ass so fat, I'm not surprised by that at all. Get your act together, Dale. I know you're having a hell of a week, but you need to resume functioning."

I yawned, stretched, and considered grabbing my boss's pillow and shoving it over my head. "It hasn't been that bad."

"Really? I find that hard to believe."

"She said I don't have to quit."

"Why would you quit?" Jerome paused and sighed. "Oh, right. No, you don't. The CDC should accommodate you two love birds, I'm sure. If you're leaving the singles market, I recommend you take the rest of the week off. She'll wear you out and then some. Also, I have been told from a very good source if you do a swapping blood transfusion, one bag each, you'll give your mating bond a good jump start. Of course, you'll need to get in a few rounds of actual mating in first, but I'm sure Allison wouldn't mind doing the transfusions."

"I'm not his blood type," Ethel growled.

Allison bounced into the bedroom. "That's why you have to get in a few rounds of mating first. Establish the mating bond and the virus will take care of the rest. I'm available tomorrow afternoon before work if you two decide to get it on and need a boost to your bond. You could send him back to his contracting work on Thursday morning. Also, I find it amusing you know his blood type."

"It's my job to know."

"Sure it is. Because you know the blood types of all your contractors?"

My boss's face turned a suspicious shade of red. "Allison!"

"I'm really good at getting people to tell me my name. I think it's a magical power. Do you think the CDC will upgrade my rating, Jerome?"

"Keep dreaming, dear. Stop butting in. I was trying to get them to take the entire week off."

"Ethel is involved. She's not going to take an entire week off. She'll fret over work, then Dale will get worried and start fretting, then we'll have to deal with them being anxious."

Either I was still asleep and dreaming or my life had taken a sharp left into the weird unknown. "Say what?"

Allison glared at me. "Dale, quiet. I'm busy making certain you're happily mated by the end of the week. You've got the relationship skills of a train wreck."

I sighed, shook my head, and considered getting out of bed and finding a quiet, private place to shift and get dressed so I wouldn't have to put up with the alphas on a mission, no matter how much I liked the idea of them succeeding at their twisted plan. "Train wrecks don't have relationship skills."

"Exactly. Now shush. Ethel, you're going to have to use a blunt bat on him. Until you get him to per—"

"Control your mate!" I howled, twisting to swipe at Jerome as Allison would kick my ass into next week. I got tangled in my boss's blanket and crashed to the floor, the breath whooshing out of my lungs.

My boss crouched beside me. "You okay, Dale?"

"Please make them stop," I begged.

"No, I don't think so. He's right. So is she. You're denser than a rock." Smiling, she patted my head. "It's okay. We can take our time. I need to get you to call me by my first name, which will be a challenge. As long as you're aware I'm claiming you, I can be patient."

Jerome crouched beside me and poked my nose. "Please let her claim you. Maybe she'll stop wearing that damned wolfsbane perfume all the time."

I flattened my ears. "I like her perfume."

"That's because you're stubborn and obsessed. The rest of us don't like it. It burns our noses. I would've brought her into our pack years ago if it weren't for that damned perfume."

My boss chuckled. "Once I've staked my claim and the CDC has a chance to evaluate how it influences our mating bond, I'll stop using it. It's just part of the test study to see what happens if I express interest in a male. If it prevents the mating bond from taking hold, we'll submit the test results and I'll stop using the perfume. We might need to borrow you for testing, Jerome."

"Spray that shit on me, and I will dump your ass into the harbor, Ethel."

"Like hell you—"

My boss clamped her hands around my muzzle. "Down, Dale. No killing Jerome in my trailer. My trailer won't survive if you romp with him in here."

"I'll keep an eye on you and sniff whenever I see you. When I notice anything, I'll tell you. Really, I'll have to watch Dale. For someone as hopeless as he is, there are a lot of ladies who've asked me if he's available. He just has no interest in anyone," he complained.

I had plenty of interest in someone, but I still had a lot of thinking and planning to do before I could move to the next stage, which involved accepting her claim.

Thinking of her as Ethel rather than my boss rose to the top spot along with finding a new place to live coming in as a close second.

Allison snickered. "There's nothing wrong with being last but not leashed. Hell, half the time I wish I'd waited before I got leashed to this lout. He's a pain in the ass. I'm pretty sure Dale will be a far superior male, Ethel."

"Allison," Jerome complained.

"You deserve it for teasing him so much. I swear, you're the pack's worst gossip sometimes. Ethel is perfectly capable of figuring out how to stake her claim before someone else does."

I eyed the bed, wondering if I could cram myself beneath it. Cursing my eight hundred pounds of bulk and muscle, I redirected my gaze to the door and contemplated staging an escape.

As though sensing my intentions, Ethel sat on my back. "I'm sure I can. Thank you for bringing his clothes over. Do you two have any other unasked for advice?"

"Feed him and send him home tonight so he can relax in his territory," Jerome replied.

"I'll keep that in mind."

"Please do." Jerome hopped to his feet. "Oh, and Ethel?"

"What?"

"Don't worry about Dana. She has more issues than National Geographic, but she does mean well. She just feels guilty she jumped on Pete and dumped Dale like he had the plague. Pete had his first-shift flare, which attracted her. Now she tries to be all politically correct around Dale, and it annoys the pack because she upsets him every single time. He's sensitive."

"Dana had her chance with him. She's got plenty of

puppies to worry about, so she can keep her attention away from him," Ethel snarled.

"Please don't put Dana in her place, however much she deserves it. It'll upset Mr. Sensitive, and when he's upset, the entire pack gets riled up. Honestly, our pack is so damned stable because we don't want to upset him. Had I known Mr. Sensitive's issues stemmed from the color of his fur, I would've done something about it already."

I growled at Jerome, earning another swat to the snout.

"If you say dye, I'll hit you."

I liked the idea of Ethel smacking Jerome around enough I pricked my ears forward and held my breath.

"No, we won't dye him. We'll be more aggressive about him coming out to play as a wolf, though. We'll also push harder to get him to hunt with us. On our next hunt, I'm expecting you to come with us. We can bring you into our pack sometime in the next few days, too. No more of your lone wolf whining nonsense. Dale won't be able to handle you being outside of the pack if you're seriously pursuing him. That should get him moving in the right direction."

"How about your pack join me for a hunt for the lycanthrope who attacked Mr. Jones? He's consented to a transfusion of his future-mate's blood; fortunately for them, they're the same blood type. It should ensure he contracts her virus instead of his attacker's. But we can't let this lycanthrope hunt people. My boss believes Dale fits the profile, so he'll be working the mall, and it's my job to make sure there's a team watching Dale and is ready for the pickup if this lycanthrope shows up."

I wasn't looking forward to the foreseeable future, although there were perks, including close proximity with the woman I desired as much as my virus did. I listened, tense beneath her, waiting for Jerome to decide what to do.

"We're in. I'll ask around the pack and see about setting up a shift to keep an eye on him. Some rogue lycanthrope taking off with one of my betas would make me the laughingstock of the entire state."

"Good. I'll talk with my boss and put together a compensation package. We might be able to arrange contractors to cover shifts, too. The attack on Dale is being viewed as a direct consequence of the attack on Mr. Jones, so it's under CDC jurisdiction. The pack, which lives a few towns over, is responsible for paying for the neutralizer we used, but they're on a payment plan."

Jerome grimaced. "Ouch. How much is that going to ding them?"

"We dumped ten thousand down the drain making sure no one contracted Dale's virus. They have a twenty-member pack, so it works out to a reasonable amount per person. It's a token slap, but the boss thought it was necessary to remind them they really shouldn't go hunting other lycanthropes and putting the public at general risk. It was her second shift as a hybrid, but her virus levels aren't anywhere near as high as Dale's."

"All right. After we take care of this situation, we'll do a proper pack hunt, and I'm expecting you to bring Dale out in a fur coat. I don't care which version of his fur coat, but there will be no getting out of it or tagging along as a human anymore. Understood?"

"I hate you sometimes."

Ethel scratched me behind my ears. "It's okay. I'll protect you."

Jerome cackled. "Someone has to protect you, Dale. You

fight like shit—and we'll be addressing *that* problem starting on Friday morning before you go to work. You got your ass handed to you."

Damn it. "It's not like I get into many fights as a wolf."

"You don't get into any fights, period. You need to be able to protect yourself. We aren't going to be able to hide you have access to the hybrid form for long, and that means you need to handle whatever anyone tosses your way. Friday morning at six. Go ahead and try to run. That'll make this even more fun for me."

FOUR

You lycanthropes really are tough, aren't you?

ETHEL SEEMED MORE than ready to stake her claim on me in a very permanent and intimate way, but I had a mile-long list of things I needed to do first. In another rare show of solidarity, my virus agreed with me.

Miracles could happen—or my virus recognized I meant to accept her claim, but I'd do so under my own terms. Before I accepted everything she offered, I needed a proper home, one capable of handling two lycanthropes at their worst. I expected once I unleashed my virus and allowed her to do whatever she wanted with me, we'd cause a great deal of property damage. I doubted my apartment or her trailer would survive our enthusiasm.

The virus came with many benefits, and endurance topped most lists.

If we trashed the home I offered, repairing it would keep me busy and help contain the other problems associated with being infected with the virus. Despite Jerome's teasing, I understood relationships took two, and while the virus would ensure loyalty to each other, it didn't necessarily make for a happy home.

I wanted it all, and I wasn't going to ruin it being an impatient idiot.

Investigating the CDC's stance on mated pairs in the workplace would need to be done quietly; my boss's boss would be the best resource, as it'd maintain the chain of command and make it clear to the CDC I was serious about her. I'd also have to work harder at not just thinking of her as my boss but as both my boss *and* Ethel. On that front, I expected few issues.

Escaping her would be the true challenge. Every time I turned around, she watched me with the sort of smile that made her difficult to resist.

But as she promised, she waited.

Her waiting made resisting her almost as difficult as her smile.

With a little help from Jerome, who showed up at her trailer in the evening and drove me out by force and with a few snarls, I got some much needed sleep in my own apartment. I'd never been so relieved to return to work, although my good mood didn't last long.

Mr. Coolridge ambushed me the instant I walked through the office doors. "You lycanthropes really are tough, aren't you?"

Why had I dodged Ethel's attempts to claim me? If I'd just gone with it, we would've been cuddled together somewhere, somewhere far away from the mall and the unwanted interest of the mall's head of security. "It's one of the advantages of being infected, sir."

"A regular man would still be in intensive care." Mr. Coolridge circled me, making thoughtful noises in his throat. "There's not even a bruise left on you. I'm impressed, son."

In the future, I would go out of my way to remind myself there were far worse things in life than Ethel's attention. I had no idea how I'd make the adjustment to having her in my life as more than my boss, but it beat dealing with Mr. Coolridge.

I cursed my professionalism and work ethic. Had I been a little more relaxed about my job, I would've come up with an excuse to turn around and head to my boss's office, tail tucked and prepared to face her wrath.

Mr. Coolridge gave me a serious case of the creeps.

"Will being on the outside round tonight be a problem for you?"

If I got mauled by another lycanthrope again, I'd have a serious problem with it, but the rules of professionalism—and my job description—stated I wouldn't express my misgivings over my assignment. "Not at all, sir."

"Good. There's a new jacket for you in the spare locker. Expect a busy day; we're down two men for the afternoon and evening shifts."

Quitting once again rose to a high priority. Monday with a full security roster had been busy. On a Thursday, I expected far worse. As perspective mattered, I took some consolation it wasn't Friday or the weekend. "Understood, sir."

"You'll be at the food court until eight, then you'll be making the exterior rounds. Have a good shift, Mr. Jameson."

From past experience working security in shopping centers, the food court patrols were the ones most likely to sour. Rowdy teens often took the top spot for causing trouble, especially if they'd recently developed magical talents. Sometimes, their trouble was accidental in nature.

Where the weird and weirder gathered in large numbers, strange shit happened.

I'd consider it a win if I went through my shift without becoming petrified.

Unlike the rest of the security staff, I kept my personal possessions with me. My wallet had seen better days but had survived Monday's excitement. My phone hadn't, so I carried a loaner from the CDC until they replaced it, which would happen sometime next week. Despite having spent an entire day trying to give Ethel the slip and provoke her into seeing how far she'd go to keep me close, I hoped she'd call with a reassignment.

Until the rogue lycanthrope was caught, I'd be spending a lot of time at the mall. If my shift went as I expected, the chaos in the food court would exhaust me within an hour.

I put on the mall security jacket, grabbed a portable radio from the box, tested it to make certain it worked, and armed myself with a spray can of neutralizer and a billy club. I hoped I wouldn't need either, but if I did, I'd be set.

Fighting as a wolf didn't work out well for me, but I'd grown up playing baseball, had good aim, and enough strength to turn the stick into a lethal weapon if needed. It didn't offer me peace of mind though, not in the way many claimed being armed did, but if something did go wrong, Jerome wouldn't have another reason to tear strips out of my hide.

The food court was on the mall's second level, a decent hike from the mall's central hub. The majority of the shoppers were human—or at least looked human—which boded well for my shift. While humans could cause trouble, they often lacked the firepower of the other races. Incubi and succubi ranked fairly high on the list of troublemakers, but most *liked* their sort of trouble.

As most of the demons enjoyed freedom, they left unmated lycanthropes alone; they didn't feel losing their freedom was worth the energy boost. However, mated lycanthropes were a different story altogether.

Succubi and incubi hunted for a pair of mated lycanthropes when it came time for them to reproduce, and as prime targets, most lycanthropes either avoided them or carried salt—not that salt was actually effective against demons. Devils, on the other hand, disliked salt. It wouldn't stop a devil, but they'd think twice about making a move.

I really hoped I didn't have to deal with demons *or* devils on my shift.

Laughter warned me of trouble in the food court, and one of the other security guards spotted me, shook his head, and intercepted me. "Coolridge sent you over? That bastard has it out for you. Good luck, Jameson. You're going to need it."

Kevin, or so his name tag declared, seemed younger than me and in a hurry to get the hell out of the area, which promised hell was about to break loose and it was going to be dumped entirely on my head. I sighed. "Thanks for the warning."

"Any time. Call in if you can't handle it. I give it ten minutes."

I nodded, straightened my back, and prepared to wade into battle, turning the corner for a full view of the food court.

A naked gorgon tangoed with a lycanthrope who lacked the hybrid form but was doing his best to dance on his hind paws. Since the floor didn't seem good enough for the pair, they took their fun to the tables. The gorgon wore tiny hoods on her snakes and a pair of sunglasses to prevent her partner from becoming petrified. Two horse centaurs gathered bets from the crowd observing the pairs antics.

I was impressed the tables didn't collapse under their weight.

What the hell was I supposed to do about a nude gorgon dancing on a table with a wolf? Did I need to do anything? Everyone in the food court seemed happy enough. A crowd of at least fifty watched the pair, hooting catcalls and goading them into taking it further than a rowdy tango on the tables.

Damn it. No matter what I did, I'd piss someone off. No wonder Kevin had been eager to dump the mess on my lap. Why was my Thursday turning into another Monday from hell? I sighed, shook my head, and pushed through the crowd. "Excuse me, miss. If you could dance with your clothes on, that would be ideal. Also, if you break any of the tables, you'll be responsible for paying for the replacements."

The pair halted and stared at me, the gorgon's mouth dropping open. She clutched the paws of her partner, as though afraid I'd claim him from her. I had no idea what she thought I'd be doing with a male lycanthrope, especially one who wasn't a member of my pack. I arched a brow and waited.

"You're not going to stop us?" she blurted.

"Unless you damage mall property or disturb other shoppers, I see no need to stop you, but I do request you put your clothes on. There might be children."

"Clothes. That's really all you want. You just want me to get dressed?"

"Please do try to avoid petrifying anyone. A call to the CDC would end your fun and likely result in a fine. As long as you keep it quiet, civil, and nonviolent, I see no reason why you can't tango to your heart's content."

If I got fired, I'd get fired for doing something amusing for once in my career. I'd have a really interesting report to file, but a chance to watch Ethel's expression as she realized I'd tossed common sense to the four winds would be worth it. If my decision to toe every last one of her lines didn't trip her trigger, I'd be cautiously optimistic about having a bright and long future with her.

I'd never truly tested her limits.

I'd never viewed it as an option before.

A cautious wolf lived longer, but games were a way of life for lycanthropes, and I had every intention of pushing Ethel's buttons to discover what would happen.

The gorgon giggled. "Want to dance, handsome?"

"Sorry, miss. I'm seeing someone." I toed the line with the truth, but I didn't care. I couldn't remember when Ethel had ruined me for other women—of any species—but I decided it didn't matter. I liked being ruined for other women, and it wasn't just my virus's fault.

I'd been born that way. I blamed my mother for it more than my father. My mother was the jealous type and hated when anyone other than my father got too close to her, and according to every gossip I knew, she'd been that way before contracting the lycanthropy virus from my father.

"That's no fun. You sure?"

"I'm sure. Try not to break any laws; I'd be forced to act." I glared at the congregation of spectators, leveling a glare at a table loaded with pixies. "No dusting." I just shook my head at the centaurs; they were likely wise enough they should at least attempt to hide their illegal gambling operation. The lycanthrope got the majority of my scrutiny. "No spreading the lycanthropy virus. In fact, none of you do anything that requires neutralizer, please."

Already regretting my decision to ignore the odd party, I pointed to the far side of the food court. "I'll be over there. Please don't need me for anything."

A FULL GORGON HIVE, including a herd of young children, joined the party, and they had two males with them. The middle-aged one was likely the hive's leader and the father of the herd, as the children clung to him while the mature females joined in the festivities. The other male looked like he already had one foot in the grave and wanted to watch the world burn before he gave up the ghost.

The children enjoyed crawling over the males, who stood on guard.

The tables that weren't bolted down had been relocated to the sides along with the chairs, allowing the hungry shoppers to dine with a good view of the mass of people determined to get in exercise on mall grounds.

To add to the chaos, as my day obviously hadn't been chaotic enough, members of my pack decided to show up and transform into mall butterflies. As if being on security duty at the mall in the midst of a gorgon-infested dance party wasn't bad enough, both of the pack's other betas and their mates showed up. Sullivan and Marie would leave me alone unless I wandered too close; he didn't want to give me a chance to practice my sarcasm on him, and she didn't want to listen to Sullivan whine about my refusal to cater to her mate's delicate sensibilities.

Dan would be the problem, as he never saw a reason to take mercy or pity on anyone, and Helen would encourage him.

The pair locked on and headed straight for me.

If I ran, Dan would chase me, Sullivan would howl his laughter, and the ladies would waste no time spreading the word I was viable prey for the pack. "Whatever it is you want, the answer is no. I'm working."

Launching the opening volley probably wouldn't save me, but I'd hope for the best.

"You've been putting the moves on Ethel, so says Jerome. You don't mess around when you pick a lady, do you?"

"I haven't put any moves on anyone." If Dan wanted to believe I was the instigator—something I would be, given time—it'd throw him off my trail for a few minutes.

"You slept in her bed. Every single male in the pack is burning with jealousy right now, especially after Ethel ripped Dana a new ass earlier today. You may as well buy yourself a collar and leash, man. You're owned."

If I ignored most of Dan's commentary, I might escape unscathed. "I had a hell shift and a mauling, and as she dosed me with high grade pixie dust, she was responsible for making certain I stayed out of trouble. She decided her place was a suitable containment cell. Don't make something out of nothing."

"You're not getting away with that this time. I asked her myself. She's on the warpath to claim you. Good luck escaping. Once a bitch picks her male, she doesn't quit. You're being hunted. We've decided we're going to help her." Dan grinned and punched my arm hard enough to stagger me.

"We've also been told if we so much as giggle over your fur, Jerome will be testing out various wolf stew recipes."

"That's not what I wanted to hear today."

"We've seen pictures of you in various stages of passed out with Ethel standing guard and snarling for the camera. You're going to be even more effective as a beta now, and that disgusts me."

That was news to me. "Why would you say that?"

"You're joking, right? No one wants to pick a fight with Ethel. She's mean."

She was? While Ethel's work in the CDC put her into contact with most of the local packs, I'd never heard anything but compliments about her. I arched a brow, kept an eye on the dance party taking the food court by storm, and waited.

"Dale, she's a lycanthrope who wears wolfsbane perfume. She's crazy."

"You didn't even know she was a lycanthrope until this week."

"Not true. She's got a gorgeous white coat and a hobby of bloodying amorous males because she's only interested in you."

While I liked that Ethel wasn't shy about staking her claim on me, I wanted to strangle my co-beta into unconsciousness so he'd leave me alone so I could work in peace. "You do realize I'm working, right? Unless you want Ethel coming over here and killing me for slacking off on the job, go away."

"You're watching a bunch of gorgons dance. I mean, in your shoes, I'd just let them dance, too. You've already been petrified once this week. And pixie dusted. And mauled at the mall."

"If I buy you a leash, would you contain him, Helen? Please?"

"And lose my chance to have fun at your expense? Never. I never even dreamed you were interested in *Ethel* of all people."

"And why do you think I'm interested in Ethel?"

"You took six bags of our alphas' blood, got hopped up on the virus, and wrapped yourself around her legs. When she scratched your chin, you melted into a vaguely Dale-shaped puddle. You then slept like a rock at her trailer, requiring Jerome to go over and prod you awake. There's no way you'd do that unless everything was perfect in your little world. We're making bets over how long it'll take her to catch you."

I sighed. "You're not going to stop, are you?"

"Not until you're happily mated."

Why me? "Fine. I have things to do first, like finding a better place to live."

"I'll tell Clyde. He'll find you a good place. Ethel's a bit of a skinflint, so she won't even think about needing a bigger place. Obviously, you're the sensible half of the pairing. Plan for at least one kid. Ethel gets stars in her eyes when there are little ones under foot."

"Any other unasked for advice, Helen?" I'd have to thank Ethel for the phrasing of that question later.

"I'd need all night, and you're supposed to be working. Honestly, I'm here because Jerome threatened to skin us if at least two members of the pack aren't hanging out at the mall until you're done this shit assignment. Jerome's convinced a rival pack is going to grab you. After seeing how bad you are at fighting, he's not sure you'll ever be able to protect yourself."

"Why am I a beta again? Can I quit?"

Helen grinned at me, lobbing a punch of her own at my arm. "You can't quit your job *or* quit being a beta. Sorry. You're stuck with us. Also, it's because of your stare down. You ooze disappointment when we screw up, and damn it, it's awful."

"You punch like you mean it," Dan added "Maybe you suck at fighting as a wolf, but you're a master at the sucker punch."

"If you didn't need me to knock sense back into you, you wouldn't get hit."

"Helen keeps telling me that."

"Maybe you should listen to her. Look, I really doubt someone is going to kidnap *me*. Ethel? Helen? Hell, even Dana and Marie—there are a lot of reasons packs would want them."

"Hybrid males are in higher demand than females." Helen rolled her eyes. "Add in Ethel, and we're going to have to keep a close eye on both of you until this asshole is dealt with. Jerome's also getting into a squabble with the pack that mauled you, so that's another concern."

"Just what I wanted to hear."

"It gets better."

"I really don't want to know."

"But you do, Dale. You really do."

"No, I don't."

Helen grinned. "It'll make you feel better."

"I don't think anything you could tell me could possibly make me feel better."

"Ethel and Dana had a fight over you this afternoon. It was glorious. Dana claims Ethel is incapable of being nurturing, thus will ruin you, our most delicate and precious little flower. My mate almost died from laughter. It was a thing of beauty. I thought Ethel was going to rupture something in her head. She was very offended Dana implied you were weak."

"My fighting skills leave a lot to be desired, and thanks to Monday, everyone knows it."

"You're sweet, and you don't like hurting people. Some idiots, like Dana, assume this means you're weak."

"Dana can't stand being within ten feet of me." I sighed and wondered how I'd become the center of pack gossip. "If it'll get you to be quiet for at least ten consecutive minutes, fine. I like my boss, I'm stuck on the whole I like my boss problem, and this is because I like being a professional at work. Furthermore, I refuse to commit to a relationship until I have a proper home. Have you seen my apartment? Are you happy now?"

Helen stood on her toes so she could pat me on the head. "Very, especially as I recorded every last word for blackmail purposes."

"I hate you, Helen."

"I know. That's what makes this so much fun. Have a nice shift. Please stay out of trouble. I'm about to have my nails done. I'd hate to ruin them."

FIVE

As so often happened in my line of
work, trouble started with a pixie.

HAD I BEEN A WISER MAN, I would've remembered Murphy's Law. That the gorgon hive and their lycanthrope friends cleared out of the food court without incident should've tipped me off something bad was about to happen.

Murphy's Law always kicked in right after I experienced some good luck. It was the one thing in life I could rely on.

As I counted my problems with wanting my boss for my life-long mate as a good thing, I should've been on guard against Murphy and his damned law. While I wanted to believe no good deed went unpunished applied over Murphy's Law, I hadn't done any good deeds worthy of notice.

As so often happened in my line of work, trouble started with a pixie. The bat-winged blight hadn't been one of the gorgon groupies; his species preferred being loners, and unlike his cheery cousins, his dust was the kind likely to send someone straight into a murderous rage.

Whether by accident or design, a lycanthrope—a cat, judging from his scent—and a human got a full dose of the dark gray, shimmering powder. In the time it took me to curse, the blighter darted off.

The lycanthrope roared, and his body twisted, grew orange and black fur, and tore through his clothes. I could've dealt with another wolf, but a tiger was a whole different ballpark, one I wanted nothing to do with. The human, or what I had thought was a human, showed off a pair of pointy teeth and hissed.

A tiger and a vampire tangoing in the food court would end in bloodshed, and I didn't want to find out who would be the victor. I also didn't want to breathe in any of the gray dust, either. If I did, I likely wouldn't remember a damned thing. Part of my training with the CDC involved controlled tests of dangerous substances.

Pixie dust was good.

Bat-winged blight dust was bad.

My beautiful boss would kill me if I got a dose of it. After she finished killing me, she'd find a way to bring me back from the dead so she could kill me again.

Why was breathing necessary?

All I could do was hope my canister of foam neutralizer would be enough to keep me from joining the rampage. Expecting the worst, I gave the can a good shake, prepared for the run of my life, and stepped forward, spraying the infuriated pair in the face in hopes of limiting the damage to a lycanthrope, a vampire, and me.

I SUCCEEDED at my primary goal: the tiger and vampire were no longer interested in killing each other. Their attention fixed on me, and just like good prey did when crossing the path of predators, I ran like a bat out of hell. Running as a human wouldn't work; the tiger would catch up and sink his claws into my ass before I escaped the food court. As a wolf, I had a chance of outrunning them as long as they didn't corner me.

The tables served as blockades, buying me enough time to shift. I left my clothes a torn pile on the floor along with my abused wallet and the CDC's temporary phone. I'd get hell over that later, but living trumped keeping my CDC identification card and phone on me.

The tiger roared, reared on his hind paws, and batted a table with his paw. It crunched beneath the force of the blow, the wooden top splintering while the metal leg bent in half. If he got a hold of me, I'd regret it for however long it took him to rip me to pieces.

I gave it five minutes at most.

Two days of patrolling the mall gave me a good idea of its layout, which might save my head from a premature removal from the rest of my body. On the other end of the food court, I had the choice of diving down the escalator or staying on the catwalk over the first floor. Jumping over the rail to the level below would be an option, if I could make some distance. Unfortunately, I couldn't afford to get too far ahead of the tiger and vampire; the pair might redirect their fury to someone else.

All I wanted in life was one week that didn't involve some sort of disaster likely to end with me being mauled, petrified, or otherwise indisposed thanks to the weird and weirder.

One week without a disaster sounded like an unobtainable heaven, something reserved for those who'd done nothing but good in their lives.

As enraged lycanthropes, cantankerous centaurs, and bloodthirsty vampires weren't uncommon, the late-night shoppers had the sense to get out of my way when I came barreling down the walkway, sparing a single breath to howl, drawing everyone's attention to me. The wise ones retreated into the nearest stores and watched from a safe distance. Others took pictures with their phones, but I wasn't sure if they found me or my pursuers more interesting.

Probably both.

A bright purple and blue wolf with a tiger and vampire close behind drew attention. Forget a new job. I needed an entire new life. Unless I had a change in luck, I wouldn't have a life at all. If the pair hot on my heels didn't tear me to pieces, I had a long list of people waiting to teach me to stay out of trouble in violent ways.

Jerome would attempt to beat self-defense skills into me. Allison would help. If Ethel joined in, I'd let them.

The rest of the pack would make popcorn and watch the mayhem.

Escaping the tiger and vampire came first. If I didn't give them the slip *after* luring them away from the mall, nothing else would matter. They'd reduce me to a bloody clump of fur smeared across the ground.

I bolted towards the main hub of the mall where the catwalks narrowed and met. With a good jump, I could reach one of the other catwalks, hit the staircase down to the first floor, and head for the nearest exit.

Once outside, I could lure the pair away from civilization and run them in circles until they collapsed or the dust wore off. I bet on collapse, which led to a whole lot of problems for me. Rage would give them strength and endurance I lacked, so it was entirely possible I'd be the one to collapse first.

The fact the dust had hit them so hard and fast worried me; it meant the bat-winged blight packed a high grade, which could last for hours before wearing off. If I caught the sparkling bastard, I'd tear him apart. He wouldn't regret his choices long, and I'd enjoy using his bones as toothpicks. I wouldn't like having to pick bits of bat-winged blight out of my teeth for hours, but some sacrifices needed to be made for the greater good.

Just to be safe, I'd wait until I was somewhere private before shredding the bat-winged blight so I could rage in private.

Or I could marinade the fluttering bastard in neutralizer before I ripped him apart.

I liked that idea a lot.

The catwalk leading to the mall's central hub was clogged with shoppers, forcing me to weave through them and slow down long enough to howl to catch their attention so they'd get out of my way. When I drew close, I skidded around one of the kiosks, sank my claws into the tile floor, and jumped over the glass barricade to the other side. I slammed into the railing of the neighboring catwalk, dug my hind claws into the glass, and scrambled up and over the railing.

Someone behind me screamed.

I hoped the woman screamed because I'd just jumped between two catwalks rather than because the tiger or vampire had gotten a hold of her. Bolting for the staircase, I clawed at the floor for traction, fully focusing my attention on my goal. Glass shattered and pelted me in the rump.

Picking out the shards wouldn't be my idea of a good time, but I preferred it to someone picking what was left of me out of a tiger's claws.

Why couldn't I have been a cheetah lycanthrope? Or a horse? A horse would've been acceptable, too. Honestly, I would've been happy with anything other than a bright purple and blue wolf with zero camouflage abilities.

"Dale?" Allison squealed.

After Allison finished shredding the tiger, she'd come after me, and I'd end up in the same damned boat headed straight to the afterlife. Since slowing down or acknowledging her would send me to the afterlife faster, I ignored my alpha, plunged down the stairs, and headed for the east wing exits, which were closest to the highway.

With my luck, I'd be the one smacked by a car running into traffic, but the alternatives left a sour taste in my mouth. Lycanthropes were durable. I'd survive.

Probably.

LYCANTHROPES AND HIGHWAYS didn't mix, and I'd feel guilty later for luring the tiger onto an obstacle course of speeding vehicles, concrete medians, asphalt, and potential death. Willfully causing an accident would likely lose me my job, but if I let the tiger and vampire run loose, there'd be carnage, and I'd lose my job anyway.

No matter what I did, I'd lose.

Diving across four lanes of traffic wouldn't end well for somebody, but I did it anyway. With the pair nipping at my heels, my best bet was to head for the suburbs on the other side of the highway, which led into a forested state park. I ran along the shoulder until I spotted several transports barreling towards me.

I darted across, aware if I took a single misstep, I'd be splattered on the asphalt.

Crunch.

Since I wasn't the one having a close encounter with a truck, I kept running.

The tiger's roar thundered, and he didn't sound too far behind me. Either he'd gotten hit and refused to stop chasing me or the vampire had gotten steamrolled. If the vampire had gotten smacked, I wouldn't feel too bad about it.

He'd probably get back up without too much of a fuss. It'd just take a few blood donations and time.

Later, I could inquire about the vampire's fate and apologize for running him out into traffic while he was hopped up on a bat-winged blight's rage-inducing glitter. I'd even be nice and offer a donation, although I wouldn't let him take it directly out of my veins.

I had a guilty conscience, not a death wish.

The tiger roared again, and I plowed across the rest of the highway and began my search for a suitable place for running an enraged tiger in circles until one of us collapsed or he caught me.

The distant howls of wolves offered some hope I wouldn't have to handle the tiger alone—assuming the wolves were part of my pack. Those who spent more time with the pack could identify each other by their howls. I couldn't.

If Jerome found out, he'd insist on some variant of cruel and unusual punishment to change that, likely in the form of a pack sleepover party.

Maybe letting the tiger catch me would be a mercy.

Where had I gone wrong with my life?

With no other choice, I ran and hoped for the best.

WITHOUT MAGIC RAGE dust goading me, it came as no surprise when the tiger caught me by the tail, sank his claws into my rump, and slammed me to the ground.

Ouch.

I rolled, shifted to my hybrid form, and snagged the tiger's chest, brought my feet into play, and tossed him off. Flipping onto my stomach, I rose to a crouch, showed off my long, sharp teeth, and barked a warning.

The tiger staggered to his paws, shaking his head.

Since everyone was convinced I packed a punch, I balled my hand and clobbered the tiger between the ears until he flopped on the ground with a groan. To make certain he stayed down, I sat on him. "Bad tiger."

Someone clapped, and I growled, seeking the source of the sound.

The bat-winged blight flitted through the trees and hovered just out of my reach. "You run fast. You hit hard, too. No wonder you're worth so much. Rumor on the wire says you have a good female, too."

A nicer man would've given a little warning—or refrained from violence. I jumped, lashed out with my clawed hand, and smashed the bat-winged blight against the nearest tree. I'd start with the menace's wings, plucking them out and grinding them to powder so he'd never bother anyone, especially me, ever again.

The little bastard dropped to the ground, and I pounced,

pinning my prey between my paw. Ethel would either praise or kill me over what I was about to do, but I no longer cared.

By the time I was done, I'd be using the bastard as a toothpick. I flexed my free hand and eyed his wings. "I was hoping for my chance to do this, you glitter-winged menace."

He screamed.

I liked the tingle, but I didn't like the
choking at all.

THE TIGER STOLE MY TOY, and we fought over it, unleashing
our nastiest snarls and roars. My toy no longer made noise,
but it smelled like candy, and it shimmered whenever I
smacked it against hard objects, including the tiger's head.

Maybe if I hadn't smacked the tiger with my toy, he
wouldn't have stolen it. I grabbed my toy out of his mouth
and pulled. "Mine."

The tiger refused to let go, and my toy snapped in half.
"Damn it, you broke it."

No longer intact, it wasn't as much fun to play with, so I
slapped the tiger with it before abandoning it. Spitting out
the other half of my toy, he roared.

I shifted to my full wolf form, growled, and pounced,
snapping my teeth at him without biting.

"What the hell is going on here?" a familiar, female, and
infuriated voice demanded.

I scrambled away from the tiger and slapped my paws
over my half of the toy so it wouldn't be taken from me.

"Dale!"

I flattened my ears, hunkered down, and pulled my toy closer to protect it.

"What on Earth has gotten into you?"

"I think he's high on black dust, Ethel," a male stated, and he lifted up a large canister, gave it a shake, and sprayed me in the face, chest, and paws with pink foam. "At least the aggression's worn off."

The foam made me tingle, and I discarded my toy for the male with the pink foam. Another blast to my muzzle staggered me, and I snapped my teeth at the stream.

It went down my throat, stuck, and choked me. I hacked to get it out, and whining, I pawed my muzzle.

I liked the tingle, but I didn't like the choking at all.

"Idiot," the man muttered, shaking his head and pulling out a water bottle. "Drink this."

Like the foam, the water was pink and shimmered, and I leveled an accusatory glare in his direction. The cranky female took her canister and sprayed the tiger down, who rolled in it and kicked his paws in the air. Once he was thoroughly doused, the female picked up my toy. "This is the first time in my life I'm going to have to write 'too stupid to live' as a cause of death. What sort of idiot dusts lycanthropes and stays within reach?"

"Dale, drink," the male ordered, thrusting the bottle at me.

I snatched it with my teeth, bit down, and shook my head, spraying water everywhere. Some made it down my throat, although most of it spilled. The plastic crunched pleasantly, and I pinned my new toy between my paws and chewed it to pieces.

"Dale," the male complained.

"He probably has no clue who you are right now, Jerome. He probably won't remember any of this later, either. His evaluations on this shit are subpar on a good day. And you're definitely right, it's black dust. Damned fucking blighters!"

"Violence potential?"

"He violently plays. In human form, he wants nothing more than to wrestle or otherwise annoy us. Anything physical. When we last tested him, I recruited half the damned floor to play dodgeball with him to keep him out of trouble. He metabolizes it like standard pixie dust with a tendency to get grumpy if he isn't physically engaged. That idiot winged menace must have provoked him. He got killed being *stupid*." The female screamed her frustration and stomped her foot. "Give him another bottle to chew on while I deal with this."

She took both halves of my broken toy away, but as the male offered another bottle for me to shred, I accepted his gift and worked to reduce it to plastic confetti, too. The male crouched beside me with a sigh. "Judging from the bloody mats on your ass, the tiger caught you. How is it you're the only man I know who can get mauled at the mall twice in one week?"

The female halted, turning to face us. "If you're expecting sense out of him, don't hold your breath. The instant it wears off, he's going to be miserable."

"How sick?"

"Someone would be holding his hair if he had enough hair to hold sick, and since you and your mate couldn't keep him contained at the mall, *you* get to deal with it. Maybe shifting will help, but get him out of here first—and deal with that damned tiger."

The male's shoulders slumped, and he glared at the tiger, who still rolled in the pink foam. "Why me?"

"I've been asking myself that all day. Good luck with them, Jerome."

"You suck."

She laughed.

IN NORMAL PEOPLE, well, as normal as the weird and weirder got, pixie dust and its variants had a high without a low or a hangover. I got a double dose, and I blamed my stomach's churning for the majority of the low. Despite having pled for a swift death, even saying please, Jerome refused. Instead of killing me, he pinned me to his bathroom floor and forced bottles of Pepto down my throat.

I made disgustingly easy prey for my alpha.

"Jesus, Dale. Ethel wasn't kidding when she said you're worse than me after New Year's. Pixie dust isn't your friend. Riddle me this? Why didn't you get sick on the high-grade stuff she injected you with?"

Ethel laughed through the door. "I'm so sorry, Dale. It's black dust, which isn't the same compound as high grade standard dust. There's something in low grades of pixie dust and its variants that make him sick. Grade A or lower makes him sick enough to send home, too. He got the high-grade stuff to avoid him puking his guts out. Can I come in? Allison bought half the pharmacy and recruited me to bring it to you. How many bottles of Pepto do you plan on giving him?"

"As many as it takes to get him to stop puking. If he'd stop throwing it up, I'd stop giving it to him. Come on in. He's between waves, and I just got the last bottle I had shoved down his throat."

Ethel cracked open the door and peeked inside. She sighed, slipped inside, and shook her head. "I'm not sure this is how you're supposed to use Pepto."

"A little extra won't hurt him. It's one of the perks of being a lycanthrope. Once his stomach settles, I'll help him take a shower, get him warmed up, and get him to bed. You can shift to your fur coat and help keep him toasty. The guest bedroom has a bathroom if he gets sick again, too. How long do you think this'll last?"

"No idea. The tiger's sick, too—he's at the hospital for observation."

"What about the vampire?"

Ethel rolled her eyes. "He's currently crying he broke someone's car. He's fine. The car isn't. The car's owner is miffed she has a vampiric attachment. Turns out he's a car enthusiast and, according to him, the greatest crime he's committed in his unlife is damaging her car. It's a mess."

"But is it your mess?"

"Not yet. My boss is handling the vampire. The tiger's my problem, but I'm off the hook for tonight. He's already been questioned, and if I'm needed before tomorrow afternoon, my boss offered to handle it."

"And what about that damned pixie?"

Setting a plastic bag on the floor and shoving it out of the way, Ethel sat beside me, reaching over to pat my back. "He was a cave nymph practitioner. He had a known criminal record but was out on good behavior. Rumor has it he's been working as an illegal bounty hunter, and the current theory is he dusted the tiger and vampire to make Dale an easier mark."

"That didn't work out well for him."

"I don't think he anticipated Dale could jump fifteen feet.

I'm pretty impressed. We found evidence you'd smacked the nymph into a tree trunk. The dust marks are fifteen feet from the ground."

I groaned and considered taking shelter in the bathtub. "If he hadn't ruined my shift, I wouldn't have hit him."

"Somewhat coherent now?"

"Jerome refuses to kill me. Tell him he should kill me. It'd be a mercy."

"I know. I heard you through the door. I'm sorry. You'll feel better soon. I brought some high-grade neutralizer with me. Maybe it'll help. Anyway, I thought you'd like to know you're cleared on the nymph. The tiger already testified to an angel that you were provoked and the little bastard had dusted a public place. It seems you flew off the handle when the nymph mentioned your female."

Busted. Ethel sounded too happy for my comfort, but after a few moments of thought, I decided it was a good thing. "He said something about me being valuable, I think. It's a bit of a blur," I admitted.

"So your new friend said. Anything I can do to help?"

"If you want to hold his hair if he throws up again, that'd be great."

I didn't have enough hair to worry about, and I shot a glare at my alpha, who grinned at me. "You're an ass."

"I am, but it's why you like me. How much Pepto did you get? And what new friend? Dale's not allowed to have any new friends right now."

Ethel pulled the bag to her and emptied it onto the tiles. "Don't get so territorial without hearing the whole story first. The tiger lycanthrope is Dale's new friend. He's unmated, and he had his first shift a year ago. He recently moved into the area. Apparently, he's not the loner type, and he's interested in joining a pack. A lot of other lycanthropes are scared shitless of him because he becomes a tiger who weighs four hundred pounds. He likes that Dale isn't instantly terrified of him. Expect him to ask about joining the pack. He requested contact information."

"And you're certain he isn't an accomplice? Does he have a name?"

"Alto, but if you have any mercy in your body, you'll call him Al. He's no threat to Dale. I asked, and an angel confirmed he had nothing to do with the situation. He was just at the mall to have some dinner, and the vampire asked if he'd donate. That's when he got dusted."

"Wait, the vampire was asking if this guy would donate?" Jerome gaped at Ethel. "At the mall?"

"Al supplements his income donating to vampires, and he meets contacts at the food court. It's legal. He's comped by the vampires, *and* he has a certificate from the CDC as a valid donor, so he doesn't have to claim his earnings on his taxes. Works well for everyone. He won't be cleared to donate for a week just to be on the safe side, but since he's an official donor, the CDC will cover his vampires until he's clean of black dust."

Ethel dug out five bottles of Pepto and lined them up beside me, and I groaned at the thought of being subjected to more of the vile medication. "You're not dying, Dale."

"According to him, he is." Jerome laughed, grabbed one of the Pepto bottles, and poked me with it. "If you don't want this shoved down your throat, stop throwing up."

After digging into one of her pockets, Ethel placed a tiny vial filled with shimmering pink powder beside the line of Pepto waiting to torment me. "This is the best neutralizer I could get on short notice. If you think he can keep it down, give him the whole thing."

"You could just put me out of my misery."

"No can do. I'm planning on keeping you around for a long time, so I can't kill you. Sorry. You'll feel better within a few hours. If you can keep it down, I'll get some water so you can take the neutralizer. Maybe it'll spare you from another round of the Pepto."

"No promises, but I'll try if it means I can avoid more of Jerome torturing me."

She laughed, hopped to her feet, and left long enough to fetch a glass of water and a spoon. She stirred in the powder until I had yet another pink beverage to drink, and I had no doubt Jerome would force it on me if I didn't drink willingly. I took consolation in the fact it tasted a hell of a lot better than Pepto did. I took several deep breaths to steady my nerves and order my rebellious stomach to settle, then I guzzled the neutralizer so it could work its magic and finish purging my body of the nymph's dust.

My tongue went numb, and realization I'd been tricked sank in. Few sedatives worked alongside neutralizer, but the CDC's favorite could flatten a human for days and was used with their glass coffins.

It also held the world record for fastest acting time.

"That was underhanded," I admitted, setting the glass down before I dropped it onto the tiles. "Cheater."

Ethel smiled and patted my cheek. "Good night, Dale. You'll feel better in the morning, promise."

I slumped against Jerome, struggling to keep my eyes open so I could glare at her for tricking me.

"Damn, Ethel. That was cold."

"Unconscious is better than sick. You get him tucked into

bed and watch over him until I get the rest of my work done."

"You got it."

"Cheater," I said, determined to get the last word in before the neutralizer and sedative cocktail did its work and the lights went out.

DAN WAS RIGHT. I found Ethel beautiful as a woman, but her sleek, pristine white wolf stole my breath and revved my virus's engine. It was a good thing I'd spent years resisting my interest in her. It made fighting my virus's insistence I do some claiming of my own easier. Had she been human, my alphas would have many reasons to be annoyed with us in the morning. I'd be forced to burn their sheets to hide our evening activities, as there was no way to hide the scent.

Worse, first matings had a reputation of being noisy, lengthy affairs. My virus wanted me to find out how noisy we could be, and if I let it have its way, we'd do a lot more than make some noise.

My virus either needed to be leashed or encouraged, and I wasn't sure which.

While Ethel slept, I slipped out of bed and investigated Jerome's guest bedroom, discovering one of my gym bags stuffed full of my clothes near the door. Dressing helped contain my virus's urges, as clothing meant things other than sleep and mating, particularly food. My stomach growled a reminder that I hadn't filled it in a long time.

I ignored it, got dressed, and took a few minutes to sit on the edge of the bed beside Ethel, running my fingers through her fur. Unlike mundane wolves, lycanthropes could have fur—and hair—of all textures and lengths. Ethel's silky coat ensured I'd be spending an inappropriate time stroking her.

My fur was thick and soft enough, but hers put mine to shame.

Ethel cracked open an eye and, without any other warning, shifted to her human form, wrapped her arms around my neck, and locked lips with me.

Okay.

I could work with that.

Who needed breakfast—or any other meal for that matter? If she wanted to defile Jerome and Allison's guest bedroom in the best way possible, I'd accept the unexpected change of plans.

My virus agreed.

She broke our kiss, smiled at me, and flopped onto the bed. Within moments, train-like snores thundered from her. I had no idea what was going on or why, but I needed a cold shower or an excuse to wake her.

I poked her shoulder, and she didn't even twitch.

I'd heard of sleep walking, but sleep kissing was a new one. I'd have to work on my kissing game, as the next time she engaged in an act of sleep kissing, I'd be ready to wake her in the best way possible. Biting my lip so I wouldn't laugh at myself and my virus's insistence I had the right idea, I covered her with the blanket and tiptoed to the door to raid my alpha's kitchen.

Kitchen raids worked a lot better when most of the pack wasn't crammed in the kitchen, dining room, and living room. I stopped counting heads at twenty and sighed. "What's going on?"

Allison bounced to me, stood on her toes, and kissed my

cheek. "You're up earlier than we expected. How are you feeling?"

My stomach voiced its complaints, and I ignored it, replying, "I'm fine, thank you."

Allison grinned. "Hungry?"

"I could eat."

"We'll try you on chicken soup. Ethel will murder us if we get you sick again. She finally settled down?"

As I tried to be a gentleman, I'd make certain no one found out about the sleep kissing incident from me. "I assume so. She's asleep."

"I hope she stays that way. She got pretty snappy and territorial after Jerome dragged you to the guest bedroom." Allison evicted several members of the pack from the kitchen and pointed at the island until I snagged a stool and sat down. "We have questions, sir."

"Just what I wanted to hear before I've had coffee."

"You may have some tea. Coffee might make you sick, and I value my life. You get soup and tea. If you don't like it, wake Ethel and take it up with her."

As far as threats went, I considered Allison's fairly potent. I wasn't sure I wanted to get a full dose of Ethel fresh from sleep and grumpy enough the rest of the pack worried for their lives. "I think I'll pass."

"Wise man."

"What are your questions?"

"What the hell did you do to get a half of a million dollar live bounty?"

My mouth dropped open, and for a long moment, I stared at her. "*What?*"

"You're worth half a million dollars. Ethel's bounty is for

a hundred thousand dollars, and it's conditional: they only pay out if you're also captured, and the terms are pretty strict. Ethel isn't to be scratched. Yours is a live bounty, but if you need to be beaten into submission, that's okay, as long as you're not disfigured. Someone really wants you, and we want to know why."

"You're serious."

"I guess you have no idea why someone would pay so much for you, do you?"

"I have no idea. Insanity?"

"So, there's no scorned lovers in the wings?"

"Why would you come to that conclusion? Absolutely not."

She grinned at me. "Jerome thinks it's because of your fur color and access to the hybrid form. You're an exotic."

"I don't exactly advertise either," I growled. "I've been careful."

"Until your first mauling at the mall, yes. The bounty was placed on Tuesday morning."

"That's just what I wanted to hear."

"We have a suspect list."

"Is it something a conspiracy theorist would concoct?"

Her grin widened. "Maybe."

"Not interested."

"Don't be a spoilsport."

"Still not interested."

Allison huffed. "Fine, be that way. It's likely one of the employers on one of your contract jobs is behind the bounties. It's not unheard of for an exotic CDC contractor to be targeted, and anyone with a passing knowledge of lycanthropes would go after Ethel to control you. That your price tag is so high indicates you're the one the buyer wants. What other tricks do you have?"

"I don't. I was as vanilla as the son of a lycanthrope gets before infection. I didn't develop any other abilities after infection."

"That you know of. Have you checked?" she challenged.

Why did I like Allison too much to actually strangle her? "I'm a lycanthrope. I don't need any other abilities."

"But what if you could fart rainbows?"

The rest of the pack choked on their laughter, and I glared at the bastards. If they woke Ethel, I'd practice my non-existent fighting skills on them. I growled a warning. They ignored me.

Bastards.

"Come on, Dale. You can't tell me you've never wanted to develop a cool ability. How about shooting lightning out of your hands? That'd be so fitting for you."

"I hate you, Allison."

"I thought you hated Helen."

"Now I hate you, too."

"Don't lie, Dale. You like us all, but you're too shy to admit it."

I sighed. No matter what I said, she'd find some way to win. Surrender would limit the torture, although I expected the pack would enjoy ganging up on me and pushing my buttons because they could. "Sure, Allison. I'm too shy. And no, I really don't want to fart rainbows *or* lightning."

"I didn't say you needed to fart lightning. I'm not that cruel. Shooting it out of your hands is good enough. But seriously? What about the lightning?"

"No."

"That's just shocking."

Like a twig under foot, I snapped, shifted to my hybrid form, and roared.

Allison cackled her laughter and ran.

Could you please stop taunting the cranky hybrid?

THE PACK SIDED WITH ALLISON, and they worked together to keep me from mopping the floor with our alpha. A pair of human shoes named Jerome and Clyde restrained me, although I had several other annoying lycanthropes hanging onto my back. Of my living shackles, Clyde enjoyed his job the most, laughing whenever I tried to kick him off. Jerome cursed me for refusing to obey him, and all of his orders boiled down to leaving Allison alone.

When she left me alone, I'd leave her alone, and she refused to stop laughing at me. "Allison!" I howled.

"Could you please stop taunting the cranky hybrid?" Jerome complained. "Holding him back isn't easy, babe."

"You both need the exercise. Don't be a baby. I'm helping. We're learning a lot about Dale's hybrid form. He's got to be dragging around a thousand pounds trying to get a hold of me, and he's been at it for half an hour. He's strong and has good endurance. That's worth the bounty price *before* considering how pretty he is. Look at him, Jerome. He's beautiful."

"Stop flirting with Ethel's future mate. I'm starting to think you have a death wish."

Allison walked backwards, keeping just out of my reach. I swiped a claw at her, and Helen joined the fray, dangling off my arm. Since biting her would earn me a beating I'd never forget, I showed her my teeth and breathed in her face.

She dropped off my arm and backpedaled, clapping her hands over her nose and mouth. "Fuck, your breath!"

"And he has weapon-grade morning breath," Allison added. "That's a potential plus on the bounty front."

"You really have a death wish, don't you?" Jerome growled at his mate.

"I already told you I just wanted to see what we have to work with. He's even better than I thought. If I had a death wish, I'd contact the bounty—"

"*No*," the entire pack chorused.

I halted to catch my breath, considering how to rid myself of my living attachments so I could mop the floor with Allison. Considering the idea of turning myself in for the bounty put me in the same looney bin as my alpha, but it had some merit. With a little preparation and some supplies, I could make a few elementary runes to help me escape if needed. Practitioner tricks were taught to most CDC contractors and employees, although I'd limited my knowledge to the basics.

After I finished mopping the floor with Allison, I'd reevaluate my stance on practitioners and their magic. A few extra tricks up my sleeve couldn't hurt.

"Allison, so help me, if you give Dale any dumb ideas, I

might just let him loose to see what he does with you. Don't you give Ethel any dumb ideas, either!"

Sometimes, I liked Jerome, but I wouldn't admit that to him.

"What dumb ideas?" Ethel demanded.

I straightened, pricking my ears forward at the sound of her voice. Allison took advantage of the opportunity to hide behind the one woman who'd held my attention for years.

"I was thinking we could get Dale to lure out the bounty holder," Allison replied with an unrepentant grin. "I think it's a great idea. Once the bounty is gone, you can live happily mated with Dale."

"I like the happily mated with Dale part of your idea, but you're going to have to do some serious convincing regarding the rest."

I sighed and bowed my head, my last hope of sanity leaping out the window with Ethel's reply. "Who would pay half a million for *me*?"

Ethel locked onto me with narrowed eyes, stomping over so she could prod me in the chest. "Me!"

Not only did I like her answer, it gave me a unique opportunity I couldn't allow to slip away. I flashed a canine grin. "Are you the bounty holder?"

"Well, no. I admit, I wish I'd thought of it first. I'd spend more than that to keep you."

I'd have to do a little investigating of my own; if I judged by Ethel's trailer, she'd never be able to afford my bounty. The way she spoke led me to believe she really would spend more and she wouldn't even hesitate.

Someone likely squirreled away every extra penny she got her hands on, and I wondered why. CDC management had to be paid better than I was, and I wasn't a slacker on earnings.

Interesting.

"My question stands," I replied, careful to keep from growling, as I didn't want to give her the impression she'd stirred my ire. That honor belonged to Allison.

"Dale," Ethel growled.

"Ethel." In light of new information and her display of aggression, I ditched any pretenses of maintaining a pleasant demeanor. If she wanted to match me growl for growl, I'd deal with the consequences. My growl was a great deal louder than hers, which annoyed her into scowling at me.

"Please don't provoke him, Ethel. He's hard enough to hold back as it is," Jerome complained. "Please. He already wants to pummel my wife."

"Why?"

"She punned him."

"Why are you trying to stop him? It sounds like she deserves it."

"I don't want her to die because she angered Dale. She provoked him right into his hybrid form."

"You should be admiring him rather than saving your wife. He's lovely."

Jerome sighed. "You're biased."

I was okay with her being biased, but I didn't want to hear them sing my praises when all I wanted to do was accomplish my mission of mopping the floor with Allison. To distract them, I said, "I still want to know who would spend that much on a bounty for me."

"You're lovely, so a lot of people should," Ethel replied. "Handsome. Vibrant. Also mine, and I'm pissed they came up with the idea first."

Jerome snickered. "You can't win this one, Dale."

Yes, I could, and I knew the perfect way to. "Hey, Jerome?"

"Should I be concerned?"

"Not particularly."

"What, then?"

"Who likes Ethel enough to pay half a million for me?"

Silence.

The entire pack stared at me before giving Ethel their undivided attention.

The focus of my interest raised her brows, planting her hands on her hips. "I didn't know anyone liked me enough to buy me Dale. I'm not complaining if that's the case, but the people I know with that sort of money would rather annoy me than help me."

Jerome cracked up laughing, curling around my leg and beating the floor with his fist. "It makes so much more sense than someone who likes Dale helping him to land you. You're pretty, you're nice enough, and you have plenty of friends. Dale's pretty, but he's a chronic loner, so he doesn't really have a lot of friends."

I considered kicking him off and using Jerome as a mop instead of his mate. "Thanks, Jerome."

"Anytime. So, Ethel. Any candidates?"

"Maybe a few."

"Like who?"

Ethel sighed and rested her cheek against my chest, which did a good job of sparing Jerome from being kicked across his house for daring to question her. The information would be useful, and it'd gotten her to come closer, something my virus and I agreed was a good situation.

Jerome cleared his throat. "Well, Ethel? Who?"

"My father's a decent candidate, and my mother would encourage him. I think they like Dale more than they like me."

"I've never met your parents. How is that even possible?"

"They adore you. You put up with me without running away."

"Are they aware you're my boss? Not running away from my boss is part of my job."

"I told them I paid you to put up with me. That only encouraged them. They've been trying to get me to settle down for years. I was born infected, and I've been told I'm the pickiest female alive. They're convinced you might be my only hope. That alone makes it pretty probable they're the assholes behind the bounty. They'd do that. And they'd set the condition I wasn't to be hurt because they'd probably kill anyone who hurt me." Ethel took a step away from me, much to my disappointment, and wrinkled her nose. "Damned lycanthrope parents."

I understood that complaint well enough. Once my parents found out I had purple fur to go with my hybrid form, they'd probably start pulling similar stunts on a much tighter budget. "How illegal is it to set a live bounty on someone anyway?"

Ethel snorted, then she laughed. "It's illegal to kidnap someone, but it's not illegal to set a live bounty. It depends. With the right terms, it's not illegal, and the kidnapping charge can be paid off with a match of the bounty to the victim."

If my parents had the money, I could see them throwing funds at ensuring I continued the family line, although their approach would likely involve paying girls to try to befriend me and get into my pants as often as possible until I found a woman I couldn't resist.

She stood in front of me, another reason I hadn't visited my parents in a shamefully long time.

"Are you telling me that you might be the cause of all this mayhem, Ethel?"

I hoped she said yes. If she said yes, I'd have a good excuse to press her buttons, rile her up, and lure her closer with the goal of making her a permanent fixture in my life.

"My parents might do something this idiotic," she admitted.

"And get away with it?"

"I probably wouldn't press any charges if they gift wrapped you for me."

Jerome snickered. "Of course you wouldn't. You'd be too busy playing with your present. Dale wouldn't press charges, either. He'd be too busy being your present and in a mating frenzy."

Killing Jerome would get in the way of making his predictions a reality, but the thought tempted me all the same.

"That had crossed my mind, too," Ethel admitted. "I'll need to look over the bounty rules and double-check the laws. My parents typically follow the word of the law while the rest of my family would do it just to piss me off. However, no one in my family would attack a human to infect him. Those two incidents are likely unrelated."

"The timing implies otherwise," I said.

"Well, if it's my parents, they heard about the incident at the mall. I could see them deciding to do something about it." She smiled. "If my family is involved, I will enjoy murdering them. But in good news, we'll have an easier time identifying who attacked Mr. Jones and why. And my family, while annoying and deserving of death if they're responsible for this, wouldn't intentionally hire a black duster. I'm willing to bet if they're behind it, the bounty terms would've made that filth avoid the job."

"Interesting." Tired of the pack climbing all over me, I leaned forward and shook, shedding people like I'd remove water from my coat. Bending down, I grabbed Jerome by the back of his neck and peeled him off my leg. Clyde released me and scrambled out of reach. Picking up my alpha, I relocated him to his kitchen counter. "For that much money, I'd do a lot," I confessed. "Why wouldn't someone else?"

Ethel growled at me. "The terms should've dissuaded him."

Licking Ethel from chin to scalp would either annoy her even more or distract her, and I hopped forward, giving her a full dose of my breath and a rude amount of wolf slobber. She squealed and backpedaled clapping her hands over her nose. "Damn it, Dale!"

I pursued her, my laughter rumbling in my chest. After her displays of interest, I deemed it acceptable to rub my nose against the gentle curve of her throat and breathe in her scent. "Let me see if I understand this. You have how many family members willing to pay how much for me to have you? You deserved being licked for that."

Allison giggled, then she false whispered, "Dale being assertive is really creepy, babe."

Given the choice, I normally wouldn't have sacrificed my chance to nuzzle Ethel, but Allison deserved a dose of my breath, too. I pulled away from Ethel, inhaled, and roared in Allison's face.

"Holy fuck, leash him! Are you part lion? You must be

part lion. Fuck, Dale. Your breath! Brush your teeth. For the love of God and fear of Satan, brush your teeth!"

I enjoyed panting in her face and following her when she attempted to escape.

"Five hundred thousand, Dale," Ethel said, snatching a handful of my chest fur and giving it a tug. I halted, giving her my undivided attention. "Six hundred thousand if I'm captured, too. I could see them gift wrapping you for me."

"Who knew? I'm a very expensive present. If you can confirm they're responsible, then we only need to worry about who attacked the security guard and why." Ethel snorted, and unable to resist the temptation, I grabbed her by the waist and sat her on the kitchen island so she'd be closer to eye level. "Confirming the situation with the security guard is more important than a live-capture bounty."

"Like hell it is! Most lycanthropes don't attack people like that, which makes me think it was a hit—a deliberate attack. Maybe by a pack member or one of her friends? That only leads to one problem: she's verified before an angel she was going to ask him to mate with her. That's why her pack was with her. They were expecting to be introduced formally. Why would anyone interfere when nature would run its course given a little time? It doesn't make sense. What I don't understand is why someone would want to infect him with lycanthropy."

I had one idea: Mr. Coolridge. "His boss was interested in the benefits of lycanthropy, especially in a security context."

"Not him. We asked."

"Before an angel?" I asked, well aware how difficult it could be to detect a clever human's lies.

"Well, no."

"How do you know he didn't lie—or that his boss put out

the hit? The CDC has access to the bounty lists through covert ops, don't they? Have someone check."

Ethel wrinkled her nose at me. "I refuse to accept there's a criminal that stupid, Dale. I refuse. No. I refuse to even consider that a stupid criminal got you mauled."

Lycanthrope males had a reputation of being overly protective, but the females were no different. I worried what would happen if Ethel got her hands on the lycanthrope who'd infected Mr. Jones. "If we can trace the virus to its source, we can find the hire if you can't locate the bounty, right? That's assuming we can't just pull out the bounty—assuming there is one."

Ethel grunted, crossed her arms over her chest, and refused to look me in the eyes. "I refuse to believe someone would be stupid enough to infect someone with lycanthropy to have a better mall security guard."

"There's some logic, and it would let him test drive a lycanthrope, in this case, me."

"That's the dumbest damned reason to infect someone with lycanthropy I've ever heard."

"Free test drive of a lycanthrope as a security guard, option to fire an employee he potentially dislikes or doesn't think is suitable? I can see it happening. The lycanthropy virus *does* lose the infected certain rights. Mr. Jones could be fired for the infection."

Ethel bared her teeth and growled, still refusing to meet my gaze. "No, no, no."

If she found out how much I was enjoying myself, she'd probably kill me—and she'd make me like it, too. "The world is plagued with dumb criminals."

She hissed like a demented cat. "No!"

"Could be mercenaries looking to recruit," Jerome said.

Ethel's frustrated scream was enough to make me grin, and I turned to face my alpha before she caught sight of my amusement. "What?"

"It could be a mercenary outfit looking for fresh blood from the securities sector. Lycanthropes get shortchanged outside of certain fields. It'd be a great way to get new hires. Baltimore has at least five outfits, and a new lycanthrope would be an asset for them."

Ethel's sigh recaptured my attention, and I twisted to face her. She relaxed and shook her head. "There's only been one attack. I really don't want a dumbfuck criminal to be the cause of all this trouble."

"Head of mall security," I corrected.

"Dumbfuck criminal."

"Does it matter if he's a dumbfuck criminal? Doesn't it make it easier to solve and move on?"

Ethel reached for me, snagged my fur in her hands, and tugged until I moved closer. Snarling, she replied, "Unacceptable! Are you seriously telling me you're okay with having been mauled over some dumbfuck criminal with a shitty motive?"

I took my time thinking it over. The so-called dumbfuck criminal with shitty motives had gotten me into the same bed with Ethel multiple times *and* had bagged me the oddest kiss of my life. Was I supposed to have a problem with the dumbfuck criminal?

Because of the dumbfuck criminal, Ethel had her hands in my fur, demonstrating every possessive tendency of a lycanthrope out to protect her territory. I liked it enough I ducked my head and nuzzled her, breathing in her scent and savoring the undertones of her annoyance.

"Seriously, Dale? You're seriously okay with it?" she wailed.

Allison giggled and hopped up on the counter, swinging her legs. "Ethel, you're showering him with affection. Of course he's okay with it. But here's what I'm wondering. If this mall security guy wants lycanthropes, why only one attack—and why hasn't the dumbfuck offered to employ Dale permanently?"

I laughed so hard my entire body shook. "After the past two chaotic shifts, only a lunatic would hire me."

Ethel's grip on my fur tightened. "Really?"

Uh oh. I recognized my error and wondered if I'd be able to save myself from her wrath. Making my death memorable would have to do. "He couldn't afford me anyway. My current boss—very probably a lunatic—offers a good salary, good work conditions, and I hear I might be granted excellent additional benefits. I have a preference for my current boss, and I'm very picky."

The annoyance in Ethel's scent eased, replaced by something a lot sweeter and tempting. "You have my attention."

Since my slip hadn't gotten me killed, the temptation to test my luck again was too much to resist. "If I turn myself in for the bounty, would I get paid? I don't see how I lose if I get paid to become your gift. I'll even wear a bow," I crooned.

"If we can confirm my wretched family is responsible for the bounty, they'd pay you, yes. They're assholes like that."

"And if I bring you, I get paid extra."

"Essentially."

How could I lose? "With that much extra money, we could get a nice little house."

A large one suitable for many puppies.

My virus liked that idea a lot.

"We can already do that," Ethel replied.

"But it would be at their expense."

"All right. And how are you planning on delivering me?"

I had a plan? "I haven't gotten that far into my planning," I confessed.

"Wear a suit. You'll distract them that way."

"I will? Why?"

"They're convinced you're plain and uninteresting because I love my sisters and don't want to kill them. They're going to be moderately surprised you're handsome and interesting. And mine."

Meeting Ethel's family might be the death of me, but I was also intrigued by what Ethel might've told them to safeguard me from their interest. "I'm mildly concerned."

"You'll understand when you meet them."

That only worried me more.

EIGHT

Ethel's mother was the kind to handle
any kidnappings personally.

ETHEL CHOSE suppertime to be delivered to her father, the one we determined most likely to be the culprit responsible for the bounty. The other members of her family, while potentially involved, didn't live in Phoenix, a thirty-minute drive outside of Baltimore. The rest of her family lived in Towson, forming the majority of the Towson pack.

Ethel's mother was the kind to handle any kidnappings personally, and had she been the mastermind, she would've secured me, wrapped me up for Ethel's pleasure, and delivered me herself.

I wasn't sure what I thought about that. On one hand, I didn't want to be kidnapped, but on the other hand, I was an avid supporter of Ethel doing whatever she wanted with me. My damned virus really would get me killed at the rate it was going.

Then there was the issue of Ethel's sisters. It never occurred to me the reason I hadn't been assigned to the Towson area until after she had confessed that her family mostly lived there.

Until she secured me as her mate, she used her role as my supervisor to keep some of the competition away.

Lycanthrope males weren't much different.

To keep Ethel on her toes and maintain the element of surprise, I remained in my hybrid form, but I packed my best suit in a duffel bag, and Ethel took it upon herself to use a few basic practitioner tricks to keep my clothes from wrinkling. My suit wouldn't impress anyone, although it was the better of the two I had, the one I used whenever I had a somewhat formal meeting, which wasn't often.

If her parents couldn't handle my purple and blue fur, I'd find out. Either they'd accept me or they wouldn't, but I wouldn't allow my embarrassment to ruin my chance to secure Ethel as my mate.

Ethel worried over nothing, as I had zero intention of pursuing anyone else. I'd use her parents to ensure no one doubted my intentions or interest in her. I'd play their game. As they seemed to want to pay a bounty for me to make their daughter happy, I'd take their cash at the same time I took their daughter.

If I played the game right, they'd probably pay me extra to not give her back, not that there was any risk of that.

Convincing Ethel she had no competition to worry about would be the real challenge.

While I waited for Ethel to be ready, I prowled the kitchen. My contented growls worried the pack, which made me growl more, which stoked their worries. If I bared even a hint of fang, I'd have to peel wolves from the ceiling.

The thought tempted me.

Allison stomped up to me and prodded me in the chest. "Why are you so growly?"

"I'm happy."

"Wag your tail if you're happy! The growling makes it sound like you're planning on eating some—" Her eyes widened. "Oh. Dale, are you happy because you're planning to mate with Ethel in the very near future?"

I twisted around so I could get a good view of my blue-tipped tail, giving it an experimental wag. "Would I do something like that?"

"A few days ago, I would've said no. Today? I'm thinking the answer is yes. While I understand you not wanting to leave your hybrid form now that you can openly strut around, why won't you shift back to human?"

I chuckled. "I'm showing off to make Ethel's sisters jealous. I'm also showing her parents I'm not just any old wolf after their daughter."

"Don't be silly. They already know. How could they not? Ethel's been drenching herself in that goddamned perfume for years because you're the only wolf in this fucking state who likes the scent."

"I like it because she wears it."

"See? You're hopeless. She could pull out your fur and you'd like it."

I flicked an ear back. "Maybe."

"You're surprisingly honest for a jerk who refused to trust his pack because his fur is a unique color."

I flattened both my ears. "You would've laughed. You did laugh."

"You're joking, right? Only an idiot, or pack, would laugh at the huge hybrid with enough strength to throw a car. As we're pack, we're allowed. It's a rule. Unless pack, don't piss off the hybrids. Now, we *are* going to keep laughing at your fighting skills, but you only have yourself to blame for that. Improve, then we won't laugh at you."

"That's fair," I admitted.

"Of course it is."

I huffed and waited for Ethel to finish coercing Jerome into loaning her his truck, the only vehicle the pack had that I could fit in comfortably while in my hybrid form.

ETHEL RETURNED to the kitchen with Jerome an hour after dragging him off to negotiate for his truck. I had no idea where Jerome had gotten the handcuffs, collar, and leash, but I loved him for them. My tail developed a life of its own, wagging at the idea of handcuffing Ethel to me so she couldn't escape.

"Don't you dare, Dale," Ethel snarled.

My tail wagged harder, and I huffed my amusement. Since I couldn't purr, I growled, "Cuffed and leashed just for me."

Allison giggled. "Even when you lose you win, Ethel. Let the little wolfie have his fun."

"You're seriously going along with this?"

For a moment, I thought she'd been talking to Allison, but Ethel's attention was fully on me. "Yes, I am. The bounty only said to deliver us both, not how. I become rich, I'm gifted to you, we're happy." I leaned forward, showing my teeth in a canine grin. "Unless you don't want me as a gift anymore?"

She sucked in a breath. "Dale!"

"It's only thirty minutes." My grin widened. "At my mercy."

"You're something else. You're not supposed to be this enthusiastic, sir."

I huffed my amusement. "Why not?"

"You're quiet and shy."

"I think I've lost the opportunity to return to my shy and quiet life," I admitted. "As such, while Allison seems to believe there's nothing wrong with being last but not leashed, I'm operating under the expectation of retaliation at a later date. As I'm going to be leashed anyway, I feel it's important I've properly earned it."

Allison cackled, her mirth so intense she plopped off her counter and hit the floor, kicking her feet. "Y-y-you…"

I waited as did the rest of the pack.

Allison choked, shuddered, and gasped out, "You've lost, Ethel. Let poor Dale have his fun. Be glad he's willing to meet your parents."

I nudged Allison with my foot. "I'm expecting them to pay me for the privilege."

I loved the sound of silence.

Jerome shot me a disgusted look. "You're taking advantage of this mess."

"Yes, I am."

Throwing his arms in the air, Jerome turned and stomped out of his kitchen. "Fine. Do what you want. Get out of my house and don't you dare come back until the wee hours of the morning. And I will kill you if you wake us up."

I picked up my bag, slung it over my shoulder, grabbed the collar, leash, and handcuffs and held them in one hand. With my free arm, I plucked Ethel off the counter, tossed her over my shoulder, and headed for Jerome's truck before my future mate got tired of my alphas' shit and killed them both.

NINE

With a little luck, I'd have fun doing it.

ETHEL DROVE as she didn't want to pay to repair Jerome's truck, a real risk thanks to my claws. She banished me to the back seat, although I wasn't certain why I'd gone along with her orders. The front seat had plenty of space for me, my claws, and even my bag. Going along with her wishes would preserve my life for a few minutes, as I expected I'd test everyone's patience when I met her parents.

How better to learn what sort of in-laws I'd have? A few pushes, a few comments, a few toes dipped into murky waters, and I'd know exactly what I'd be getting into.

While the decision was already made, understanding the nuances of my decision to secure Ethel as my mate was important. How would I know which lines I couldn't cross unless I poked and prodded them? My fur color would establish the basics. I'd play the rest by ear.

With a little luck, I'd have fun doing it.

On the other hand, everything that could go wrong probably would, and I had doubts I'd survive when it did. Ethel alone could take over the world if she wanted, and I loved her for it. I played hard to get, but I belonged to her as much as my virus insisted she belonged to me. My delays weren't necessary, although I wanted to be in a better position to have a home before I took the plunge.

Sacrifices would be made, and I wouldn't survive another night with her without giving in to my need to make her mine in all ways—or have her make me hers in all ways. All it would take was one intentional kiss to break me.

I wondered which one of us would make the first move.

It wouldn't take her long to figure out how much power she held over me, and I'd enjoy when I finally unleashed myself around her, showing her how much I wanted her.

Then again, she likely already knew. Lycanthropes had sensitive noses.

"When we arrive at my parents' place, I recommend you cuff my hands in front of me," she muttered.

I worried. "Why?"

"I can't strangle my parents for this stupid stunt if my hands are behind my back. They should've ensured no harm came to you."

I barked a laugh. "Really, Ethel? I'm a lycanthrope male. We have a reputation of being difficult to capture on a good day, thus the bonus bounty for you. I'd like to know what you've been telling them about me for them to resort to using that tactic," I teased.

"They know I'm interested in you. They know you're one of my contractors. Little else."

A wiser man would've left it alone, but curiosity ate away at me. "Tell me more about the little else, please."

She giggled, drumming her fingers on the steering wheel. "I had one too many girly drinks with Dad, and I think I told them I liked you in your jeans so much that I wanted to rip you out of them."

I made a mental note to buy more jeans. "Girly drinks?"

"Yeah. They're girly because the manly ones leave the drinker upright when it's done with them. Daddy doesn't like when his little girl drinks him under the table."

"What the hell are you drinking that'll knock a lycanthrope under the table?"

"Cherries in moonshine."

"How is that girly? Since when is moonshine girly?"

Her giggling grew into laughter. "I dared Dad to eat just the cherries once. I was adding them to my Sex on the Beach. Knocked him off his seat. We had to carry him to his bedroom that night."

"Should I be concerned?"

"Only if you make fun of my liquor."

"I probably wouldn't say no to sex on a beach," I admitted. I could think of a few beaches within comfortable driving distance, and some were more private than others.

"Is that all it'd take?" she demanded.

I grinned. "Ask me again after I survive meeting your parents, then you'll find out."

ETHEL'S PARENTS lived in a mansion, which I should've expected considering how much they were willing to spend on their bounty stunt. The presence of seven luxury cars in the driveway, however, worried me.

Ethel pulled in behind the cars, angled the truck to ensure they'd have to drive on the grass to escape the property, and killed the engine. With breathy growls I wanted to hear more of, she pounded the steering wheel. "Damn it! All of my brothers and sisters are here."

Some things needed to be addressed, and a cranky lycanthrope female protecting her territory might level the entire mansion given a few minutes and provocation. "I'm not going to leave you for one of your sisters."

"It's my brothers I'm worried about."

Wait. What? I blinked, thought about it, but came to the same conclusion each time. I'd never understand women. "If I'm unwilling to leave you for one of your sisters, I'm definitely not going to leave you for one of your brothers."

"Dale!"

"What? It's true."

"Dale. They're not going to try to seduce you. They'll try to pick a fight with you."

Ah. "And?"

"They'll kick your ass."

I nodded my agreement with her assessment of the situation. "I'm used to having my ass kicked, but I can take a beating with the best of them. If I'm going to require transfusions, I request you be the donor."

If she didn't clue in I wanted her from that, I'd have to start spelling it out to get the point across.

"Keep talking like that, and we're going to end up having a quickie in the back of Jerome's truck," she growled.

"I deserve a bed—and not the back of a truck variety."

"Hotel?"

"We'll see."

"That wasn't a no."

"How observant of you. Should I survive my meeting with your parents, there will be no crashing Jerome's truck trying to get a hotel faster."

"You might need to drive, then."

I'd underestimated the appeal of a frustrated, desperate woman wanting *me*. "Once I'm rich, I can get a nice house for us, *and* I can pay for any damages we do to the hotel room, but I need to be rich first, which means we can't detour to a bed right now."

"I'll pay for it."

"I know you can."

"Why is it an issue?"

"Because I need to prove I can?"

"Damned lycanthrope males!"

Unable to help myself, I laughed. "You only have yourself to blame for charming my virus so thoroughly."

"Good. But I can provide for both of us."

"I know that, but I want to be a competent partner."

"I have no doubts of your competency. Except in a fight."

As I deserved that, I sighed. "That's something."

Unbuckling her seatbelt, Ethel crawled onto the driver's seat before wiggling her way into the back with me. "Leash me."

With two words, she tested my patience, dignity, and general ability to string two words together. Had I been thinking earlier, I would've seen the cuffs and leash as the traps they were. I'd spend the entire evening pretending I didn't want to use Jerome's truck to stake an intimate claim on the woman I loved.

Maybe thinking about my taxes or various brutal ways to die would get me through the evening without my scent betraying my desire. After two work-related catastrophes, my taxes would be a nightmare.

"Leash me," she whispered in my ear. "Then you can cuff me. Securely."

I growled. "You're evil."

"It's your fault you're so handsome. I have itches I want you to scratch, sir."

With her talking like that, I was done. "Where's the nearest hotel?"

Laughing, she pointed at her parents' mansion. "All bedrooms are essentially soundproofed as my parents enjoy feeding people liquor. Drunk people get rowdy. Rowdy people often decide to sleep together, and no one here wants an audience. We're rowdy but private."

"There's no way I'm surviving tonight is there?"

"They'll ply you with booze and lock you in my bedroom the instant they learn who you are. And they'll probably hold you hostage at gunpoint until I get what I want. You. In case you weren't certain."

I narrowed my eyes. "Are you sure you're not the one who's behind the bounty?"

"I'm going to make them pay for coming up with the idea first—after you're safely mated to me. For now, this benefits me. I'm going to take advantage of their idiocy. I'm willing to bet my asshole uncles helped talk my father into this."

I started with the collar, as she'd ordered; wrapping it around her throat and buckling it tested me far more than I'd anticipated. Cuffing her gave me and my virus ideas, all of them perverted. Handing her the duffel with my clothes helped remind my virus waiting was necessary.

Long enough to confirm her bedroom was soundproofed —or partially soundproofed. I could deal with partially soundproofed.

"I disapprove of this bag."

As I could see Ethel wanting to tear into her family, even cuffed, I replied, "Swing it like a weapon."

"Oh, I like that. You're not going to stop me from beating my family?"

"While I'd like to get paid, I'll accept any losses should your temper snap before they can cut me a check. Just don't hurt yourself hurting them."

If they hurt her, I'd join in the fray and lose miserably.

"Deal. A few warnings. Dad might get growly over the collar. Ignore him. If he bothers you, do that roar you do. He's a big pussy cat. Mom's the one you need to worry about."

I believed her. If Ethel's mother was anything like her, her father wouldn't need to lift a finger to keep the family safe. I'd seen Ethel armed and dangerous.

Only a fool would deliberately test her. By those standards, I was the king of all fools, as I'd do so at every opportunity.

"The sooner you get your family to pay out the bounty, the sooner we can test your claim that the rooms are soundproofed," I growled.

"They're not fully soundproofed, but as long as we avoid screaming, it'll be as private as a full house gets."

"So, not private at all?"

"I wouldn't worry about any screaming, honestly. We're lycanthropes. We're not exactly quiet by nature. They're also lycanthropes, so it's not like my family is going to care, especially not after paying so much for us to make a little noise."

I questioned her use of 'little,' but as everything else made sense, I decided against arguing with her. "The hotel probably has paper-thin walls anyway," I admitted.

"Who cares? If they put a glass to the door, they can be jealous of your prowess. I saw you first, so tough shit for them."

"You're assuming a lot."

Ethel grinned. "Basic lycanthrope biology, and every single woman I've asked has confirmed the rumor: a male in the mating frenzy is a wonder to behold. I'm looking forward to it."

So many assumptions, so little time. Some of her assumptions were correct: once I got my hands on her, I wouldn't let her go until I was certain no one would doubt she was mine and I was hers. As for being a wonder to behold, we wouldn't know until I tried, and I had no intention of disappointing her. What she neglected to say was that the lycanthrope ladies had the same reputation, and I looked forward to her getting her hands on me.

If her parents' home didn't survive, they only had themselves to blame.

AN OLDER MAN in worn jeans and a flannel shirt dozed on the porch steps, blocking the way to the front door. Ethel's patience-worn sigh worried me, as I expected her temper would fray easier than normal.

Collared, leashed, and handcuffed wouldn't do much to protect her targets. She'd find a way to turn my bag into a lethal weapon. Would the sleeper on the step survive?

I'd find out soon enough.

"Uncle Alan, why are you sleeping outside?"

"I annoyed your ma. She kicked me out, said not to come back in until you came home for a visit, and refuses to give me my keys. That damned brat of mine stole my car, too. Been here three days now, and I've been told I should be grateful she's feeding me."

"That was stupid of you."

"Didn't think it'd take a hunter so long to catch you. Gonna have to give that pack of yours some credit for keeping you so long." Ethel's uncle cracked open an eye, looked me over, and whistled. "Forget that other male, baby girl. Claim this one. You ain't gonna find a prettier one in the state. How'd he get a collar on you without you ripping his arms off and feeding them to him?"

"Uncle! This is Dale."

Ethel's uncle opened his other eye and both his brows rose. "Your Dale's a hybrid?!"

"Surprised me, too," she admitted.

"That explains the collar and the cuffs. You're making him look all fierce for my brother and his lady?"

"I think he's trying to prevent murders. Yours."

Ethel's uncle chuckled and lurched upright. "Don't get all upset over nothin', baby girl. So, son. You claimin' the bounties?"

"That's the idea, sir," I replied. "I'm going to buy us a nice house with the money."

"One good for puppies?"

I flicked an ear back and struggled to control my tail. Wagging wouldn't win me anything except some embarrassment. "One that'll survive two newly mated lycanthropes, sir."

He laughed. "If it can survive that, it should survive puppies—maybe. You took your sweet time working my niece. You planning on landing her sometime this year, or are we going to have to encourage you to get a move on?"

"Uncle Alan!" Ethel snarled and tightened her hold on my bag. "I swear, if he gets scared off because of you, no one—"

I tugged on Ethel's leash. "I'm not sure I can afford a durable house *and* bail."

"Damn it, Dale!"

"You're worrying over nothing."

Her pout tempted me into beating her uncle so I could take her off and get straight to the mating frenzy part of our day. "But I want to beat sense into him."

I wanted him to go away, but I restrained myself. Given a few more minutes, she'd need to collar and leash me. Both of us riled up would lead directly to disaster. Lycanthrope males had a reputation of being dangerous, but I'd seen the truth often enough within our pack: it often took violence or intimacy to calm a female ready to rampage. Males had the same issue, but *I* could be reasoned with—usually.

Ethel tended to stick to her guns, and she was good enough with most weapons the CDC gave her, even the big ones when needed. However, she didn't need weapons to be dangerous.

I'd have to request a pay increase for saving her uncle's life. I sighed. "You might regret killing him later, Ethel."

"Like hell I will!"

"Ethel."

"What? He's an ass. My entire family? Asses."

Ethel's uncle snickered. "Can't say she's wrong, son."

"Let's try to get through the evening without mauling anyone, please. I've reached my quota of maulings for the week."

"I don't know, Dale. Dad deserves it."

I huffed. "Before you beat your father, perhaps you should ask your uncle why he's surprised I'm a hybrid—and why they decided to issue the bounty when they did if they weren't aware I'm a hybrid."

"Huh. Never thought I'd be sayin' this, but you're huntin' yourself a smart one, baby girl. It's easy, son. She done called her ma and told her some bitch tried to run off with you. We figured we needed to put an end to that nonsense, so it's best you accept it now. It's too late to run. You're not leavin' until our baby girl gets what she wants."

Psychotic family, check. Beautiful woman worth dealing with the psychotic family, check. Approval of psychotic family, check.

My life had become strange, but I didn't mind it. Did that make me psychotic, too?

I decided to ignore all of the craziness coming out of her uncle's mouth. "Ethel, why is he calling you a baby girl?"

"I'm the oldest, so I'm saddled with it. Don't worry about it. You'll get used to it."

"Honestly, I'm more worried about another pack of angry lycanthropes beating me. One's enough for a while."

"They're not going to beat you."

"Maybe. We'll see, assuming I survive the evening without being beaten. Now, that said, you owe me. You, however accidentally, caused this mess."

Ethel sighed. "Damn it. I should've known my dumbass mother talked to Dad."

"Now, now, baby girl. Your ma just cares, and she was right worried to hear someone had hurt your Dale."

"Already claimed your territory with your family, have you?" I teased, giving a gentle tug of the leash. "I'm not that skittish, Ethel."

"Like hell you aren't!"

I laughed, shaking my head over how my drive to maintain professionalism had given Ethel the wrong idea about me. "I just wanted to maintain my professionalism at work. I've had my assumptions corrected."

"Good."

Ethel's uncle sighed. "We don't get to knock sense into Dale?"

"Touch him and I'll kill you."

"What do you got to say about that, son?"

I stared at him. "If you beat me, I'll be useless to Ethel. I think she's tired of watching me sleep off beatings."

He cackled. "I expect so. You'll anger her pappy something fierce if you tug on that leash much. Fair warning."

"I'm confident Ethel can subdue her father as necessary."

"She's handcuffed, son."

"She has the bag. That's a weapon."

"I think you're overestimating her a little there, son."

I arched a brow, reached over, and unclipped the leash from Ethel's collar. "I'll pay bail, but if I don't have enough left over, you're going to have to help with the house payments."

Ethel wielded my bag like a club and dove for her uncle.

I WAITED until Ethel's uncle begged for mercy before clipping the leash to her collar and pulling her back. "You don't want to kill him."

"Like hell I don't!"

"If you kill him, our evening plans will be ruined," I reminded her. "Bail for assault is cheaper than bail for murder, too."

"He deserves it."

The front door opened and a middle-aged man with

Ethel's eyes stepped onto the porch. "What's going on out here?"

Ethel lunged forward, swinging with my bag. Reeling her in, I wrapped my arm around her waist before standing to my full height, lifting her off the ground. "Will you stop attacking everyone? Geeze, woman."

"This is the bastard responsible for the bounty."

"I thought your mother was?"

"They're both responsible. Put me down. That bastard needs a beating."

"No."

"Put me down."

"No. If I put you down, I'll have to pay even more in bail."

Ethel's father frowned. "Alan, what's going on?"

"If you write the lad a big check, you might get some grandpups out of the deal."

I sighed.

"I only see the girl. The bounty was for that boy with the dratted girl as a bonus payout."

Ethel growled and snapped her teeth at her father. "Let me kill him."

Next time, we'd visit my family. They were saner. "No. If you kill him, I don't get paid."

"Without the boy, you don't get paid."

I displayed my fangs and growled. As I refused to call myself a boy, I replied, "I'm Dale."

"Oh. You're the boy. All right, then." Ethel's father hesitated, blinking. "Baby girl, you didn't tell us your boy was so colorful."

"I told you I'd never seen him as a wolf, Daddy!" she howled.

"That's your fault for not doing better research on your boy."

"Daddy! Damn it, because of you, a black duster went for him. For that alone, I should beat you to death."

"You're cranky," I muttered, securing my grip on her and tucking her close to me, hoping she'd limit her viciousness to something I'd survive. "I'm sorry for her, sir. She's annoyed we've been delayed."

"Delayed from what? Committing a murder?"

After so many years of controlling my expression and tone, I remained as neutral as possible considering the circumstances. "Testing the soundproofing of her room, sir, along with the general durability of your home. She wanted to forgo collecting the bounty, but I have plans for the money, sir."

"It involves a house large enough for puppies," Ethel's uncle announced.

My purple fur would cause me grief for the rest of my life, but my hybrid form granted me the strength required to mule kick Ethel's uncle off the porch. Ethel twisted around in my grip to stare behind me. "Sir."

"You punted him right off the porch." Ethel giggled. "Sorry, Uncle Alan. He's getting used to asserting himself. I'm sure he only meant to give you a love tap."

I had?

"He deserved it," Ethel's father said. "Come on in, then. I reckon one of you might start with telling me why my baby girl is cuffed and leashed."

"I begged for it," the love of my life declared with no sign of embarrassment. "He resisted at first, but I can be convincing."

I sighed again, wondering how I'd survive my first meeting with Ethel's parents.

"I think you're testing your boy's patience."

"The entire pack has been. It's been fun. He mopped the kitchen floor with Allison because she punned him. We're slowly convincing him to come out of his shell."

"Slowly?" I fought the urge to roll my eyes.

"If it means you'll stop wearing that damned perfume of yours all the time, go ahead and destroy the house tonight. It took a week for the stink to fade last time you visited. If you're going to stink up my house, may as well get to do some renovations at the same time."

Ethel wiggled in my hold. "You can put me down now, Dale."

I snorted. "If I put you down, you'll go for the throat of the next person to annoy you."

Ethel's father chuckled and turned to enter his home. "He's right, baby girl. You need to get laid before someone gets hurt."

As expected, Ethel snarled and struggled to escape my hold, determined to perform a brutal act of patricide.

I decided against telling Ethel her father was right.

Uh oh. The clean freak's emerging.

ON THE OUTSIDE, Ethel's family lived in luxury.

On the inside, I discovered Ethel's tendency to leave her laundry scattered to the four winds was either a learned behavior or a genetic defect. Did I want to ask why a pair of boxers dangled from the chandelier? At some twenty feet over head, the how was almost as important as the why. In a normal house, the foyer would've been a welcoming space.

Ethel's parents used theirs as a mud room with an emphasis on the mud. My fingers itched to clean—no, detox —the place. The marble should've been white instead of brown, and I doubted the walls would ever recover from being splattered with mud left to dry. Jackets hung from a rack and littered the floor, creating an obstacle course I'd have to navigate with care as my claws would leave confetti in my wake.

A growl slipped out before I could stop it.

"Uh oh. The clean freak's emerging," Ethel chirped, sounding too happy for my comfort. "Hey, Daddy?"

"I'm not sure I want to ask."

"I think Dale's going to use us all as mops if we're not careful. Please tell me you're not using the living room as a gun showroom again."

"Nah. It's tack day. We're doing general cleaning and repair of the leather. Already recruited your brothers and sisters to help. Your boy know his way around a horse?"

"Dale?"

"No, I don't."

"Pity. I trust you'll be fixing that, baby girl?"

"Dad, he doesn't need to wrangle horses."

"Does. What's his height and weight when he isn't sporting a fur coat?"

"Too tall, sexy, and muscular to be a jockey. Forget it. Anyway, we're going to be too busy to run him to the farm for riding lessons. We have to hunt for the lycanthrope who attacked a security guard and started this mess in the first place. We have no hits on the bounty markets the CDC has access to so far."

"He? I thought a hybrid bitch tried to take your boy."

"Damn it. Why couldn't Ma pass along the whole story right? No. A lycanthrope, a male from what we can tell, attacked a security guard at a mall. I assigned Dale to cover the next day. Dale was attacked the first night he worked the mall. The bitch was wanting to establish a mating bond with the vic and thought it was a good idea to use Dale as leverage against the CDC so she could see him."

"Dumbass. She just had to ask to see him. The CDC ain't stupid. They know separating a bitch from the subject of her interest can be a lethal mistake." Ethel's father snorted. "The guard survive?"

"He did, but he got a blood transfusion from the bitch

who attacked Dale because the CDC determined his infection probability to be over ninety percent."

"Tough luck for that guy, but that bitch should relax. You should take a page out of her book, baby girl. You even managed to lure him here. Good work."

"Dad!"

"So, what have you got on the attacker?"

"Not much. Our best lead is someone who works in mall security, wanting to get a lycanthrope to test on shifts, but that'd make it a case of dumbfuck criminal."

Ethel's father sighed. "Right. The one who requested Dale after the attack?"

"Not Dale specifically, but a lycanthrope. I sent Dale because he's the best peacekeeper type we've got."

"What, you a submissive, boy?"

"He's one of the Baltimore pack's betas, Dad."

"Boy's still got his tongue, let him do his own talking. Damn, you're just like your ma, doing all the talking for us."

"But she's right, sir," I replied.

"Don't you go encouraging her, boy!"

I needed to have a long talk with my virus about what it had gotten me into.

"Leave him alone, Dad. Anyway, this is stupid. It'll be years before Mr. Jones is useful because of his virus. I hate dumbfuck criminals!"

Ethel's father sighed. "I know you hate willful ignorance, baby girl, but that's what this is. Same shit, different day. But there's a bright side. You'll get your boy safely mated to you as a result. And don't you go knocking my bright sides like your ma."

"Your bright side doesn't find the culprit."

Shaking his head, Ethel's father replied, "A cash-strapped

lycanthrope with a common virus would do a hit like that for a grand. I can check with my contacts, and you can spread word around at work. The CDC will take steps if any more security personnel are attacked. If there aren't any more attacks, it's no longer an issue. Problem solved. Also, I'll toss in a ten grand bounty on the name of the one who put out the hit for this Mr. Jones. You said he was mall security?"

"Yes. Odds you can catch the lycanthrope?"

"Nil at best unless you got a good blood or fur sample."

"We don't. The fucker shaved and cleaned up after himself. We think he was a male because of Mr. Jones's descriptions."

I blinked. "He what?"

"Shaved, Dale. He removed his fur to limit DNA samples on the site. After the attack, practitioner magic was used to clean the scene."

Ethel's father chuckled. "The CDC ain't got a hope in hell of figuring out who done did that one. Give it up, baby girl. We'll have supper in not too long, then you can take your boy on upstairs and have fun with him for a few days."

"Dad, that would be kidnapping."

I didn't agree, but I wasn't going to get between them, especially as I wanted to be taken up to her room for a couple of days.

"I can afford the fine. You gonna put up a fight, boy?"

Since I couldn't fight them, I'd join them, and I'd toss the last shreds of my dignity out the nearest window. "I've had enough beatings for one week, sir."

"See? If he's cooperating, it isn't kidnapping. And we're not relocating him. It would be a hostage situation. Hostages don't have to be kidnapped."

"We are not going to argue the nuances of kidnapping victims and hostages. If it's against his will, it's kidnapping."

"And it doubles his payout so he can buy the house he wants. Just kidnap him and stop your whining."

"Dad," Ethel complained.

"At least go take your boy up to your room and get him into some clothes so you can help finish with the tack before supper. I'll go have your ma see if she can get a hit on your lycanthrope attack so you don't stress your pretty self on an investigation you ain't got a hope in hell of solving. I don't want your work getting in the way of my future grand-puppies."

I scowled, reevaluating my base desire to avoid paying bail, realized murder might be the only acceptable solution, and set Ethel on her feet before reaching for the leash's clip.

"You leave that on her, boy. I can't wait to see what her ma has to say about it. Do remove those cuffs so she can help with the tack, though."

"I'm pretty sure those cuffs are what's keeping her from committing a murder, sir."

"Nonsense. Our little Ethel just likes showing her affection violently."

"Maybe if you stopped annoying her, she wouldn't become violent, sir."

"That's no fun at all. Ain't you done beaten the boy on the mat yet, baby girl? He don't seem tenderized yet to me."

"Dale's fairly pacifistic," she replied, straightening and keeping a firm hold on my bag.

"Did you hit your head to pick a pacifist?"

"Damn it, Dad!"

"What? You ain't no pacifist, baby girl. You're going to drive that poor boy crazy." Ethel's father looked me in the eyes and announced, "If you need to be rescued, you just give us a call, you hear?"

I was no king of relationships, but even I grasped the basics: when in doubt, supporting my partner would keep me out of trouble. I took my bag from Ethel, hooked a claw beneath the chain linking her cuffs, and lifted. The metal survived longer than I expected before separating. A single slash shredded the leash. "Try not to kill anyone, and I meant what I said about the bail."

Ethel's father spat curses, turned tail, and ran.

IF THE HOUSE SURVIVED ETHEL, I'd be impressed. Once unleashed, she went from reasonable to a devil on a mission of destruction. Her father made it a few steps before she took chase, howling curses.

Ethel's uncle cleared his throat as he stepped beside me.

"What?" I asked.

"Was letting her loose wise?"

"I'm a firm believer of facing the consequences of one's actions."

"You don't run from her when she's pissy, do you?"

"When she's pissy, it's because I've earned her ire, thus deserve her tearing into me."

"Okay. I can see why she'd get stuck on you, then. It takes a lot of courage to stand firm when she's angry."

"It does?" I could think of a handful of times lately I'd annoyed her just to see what she'd do.

"Fair warning, son. Her ma's got enough elf in her you'll be on the menu if you hurt our baby girl."

Before I'd contracted lycanthropy, I'd been an oddity with

my unusually high percentage of pure human. When I'd undergone my evaluation, the CDC had been a little too interested in my high percentage of humanity than my parents had been comfortable with.

Lycanthropy typically rewrote and erased standard human DNA.

Such was not the case with me; I'd lost a single percentage of pure human upon infection, and my genetics hadn't changed post shift. I was as much of a freak as an elf.

In retrospect, my maintained humanity might be to blame for my unique fur color. If I volunteered to undergo additional evaluations, I wouldn't need the bounty money. The CDC would pay well for the right to poke and prod at me to figure out how I ticked.

Ethel being part elf wasn't a problem for me, although I was concerned about their reputation of eating whatever crossed their path and pissed them off.

"How much elf is she?"

"Ethel? She's a quarter, roughly."

"One of Ethel's grandparents is a full elf?"

"Yep."

"That explains a lot. Ethel looks like a full human. Doesn't her mother have lycanthropy?"

"Lucky roll of the dice; her ma turned out human enough to catch the virus. Of all the brats, Ethel's got the most elf in her. It's a good thing you're a lycanthrope. You'll survive— probably."

"I had no idea she's part elf."

"Most don't. They just figure our baby girl's a powder keg set to blow."

"Huh."

"No such worry for you, son?"

"I've never noticed. Doesn't matter to me, either." Something crashed in the other room, and I winced, hoping Ethel emerged unscathed. "Much."

"Well, don't you worry. You won't need bail. Come along. I'll show you to the bathroom so you can get changed, then we'll go have a look for some intel on that lycanthrope attack so you don't have any distractions. I figure that's what brought you two over?"

"I'm pretty sure I'm here to get paid off in advance for marrying an elf. I make decent money, but I don't make the sort of money needed for a good house for lycanthropes, puppies, *or* elves."

"Elves don't tend to do a lot of property damage. Usually." Ethel's uncle hesitated, then he sighed. "Who the hell am I kidding? Good lord, no wonder she wants you. You're so practical it's downright frightening, and she likes practical."

My father thought my practical nature was a birth defect, but after hearing Ethel liked it, I'd make a point of informing my family, loudly, I was perfect as I was. I'd enjoy it. "Good to know."

"Come along. This way. Forgive the clutter. Missy lost her temper, and when she loses her temper, the brave lycanthropes hide in their rooms until she's less murderous. Missy's been working the horses a lot, and she's trailed mud everywhere. It'll keep my brother busy once she cools off. The place needed an overhaul anyway. Hasn't been painted in at least ten years." Ethel's uncle crossed the foyer and waited for me at the start of a hallway.

I cast a doubtful look at the chandelier. "I see."

"Ah, that. Ethel's pappy tried to charm her ma into a better mood. He got tangled in the chandelier by his britches."

"Should I be concerned?"

"Only if you annoy Missy, which I doubt. Us Frankwell men have a tendency to put our feet into our mouths at the worst times. I bet Missy got upset because our baby girl was upset the lycanthrope bitch who hurt you cooperated. I heard some nonsense about a big gun and decided I didn't want to know anything else."

"Wise man. Let me see if I understand this. As long as I don't upset Ethel, I won't upset Missy—her mother?"

"Yes."

"Anything else I should know?"

"Don't run. It wakes her elven instincts."

What had I gotten myself into? As it was too late to run, I followed Ethel's uncle down the hall to a bathroom spacious enough for several people. The centerpiece of the room was a jet tub meant for two. While I locked the door, I shifted and dressed before someone decided the door needed to be replaced. I delayed long enough to comb my hair and make myself presentable.

It'd take longer than five minutes in a bathroom to manage anything other than passable, but I did what I could. Sighing, I slung my bag over my shoulder and left the bathroom's flimsy safety.

Ethel's uncle waited with a willowy waif of a woman, who watched me with narrowed, pale eyes. I'd seen the same look hundreds of times on Ethel's face when she was scheming something.

Usually trouble.

I couldn't help myself; I smiled. "You must be Ethel's mother. I'm Dale. It's a pleasure to meet you."

She blinked. "Well, damn. You've got a pair of steep balls on you, don't you?"

"Running is tiring, ma'am. Why waste the energy?"

"Smart man, especially since my baby girl has plans on tuckering you out tonight. Her pappy's running her around, and I expect it'll take him an hour or two before she's settled. Once she's riled up, she needs a good chase to work out her nerves. My fault. The other brats didn't inherit as many of my tendencies. She's just like my ma, Ethel. Last to get hitched but first for most everything else. I reckon she'll keep you busy with a little one in nine months."

Sometimes, I hated other members of my species. To take the focus off me and Ethel, I asked, "Do you have any other grandchildren?"

"My brats, save for Ethel, got themselves one or two each. You're my only hope for a full herd from one pair."

I glanced at Ethel's uncle, who seemed like the more reasonable option of the two. "I don't suppose I can negotiate the bounty up, can I? I'm going to need a lot more than what's on offer for a house capable of withstanding an entire herd of children."

Something crunched deeper in the house, and Ethel's uncle sighed. "Plus a psychotic part elf requiring exercise or sedation once a month."

"How does that rank up against a cranky lycanthrope?"

"Fairly close."

"And should any children inherit her tendencies?"

Ethel's mother tossed her head back and cackled. "Don't you worry your pretty head, sugar. My Ethel's a skinflint. She could probably retire tomorrow if she wanted, but she won't. She enjoys work too much, although I think you play a part in that. But you are what you are, and like most lycanthrope males ready to take a mate, you're driven to provide. I like that you've put aside your pride to secure what you feel is needed for your family. I see why my daughter might want you. Still, I'm surprised."

I was surprised Ethel wanted me, but I wasn't going to question the good things in my life. "Why are you surprised?"

"You're quite handsome, have the hybrid form, and you're patient. What's wrong with you?"

"I can't fight worth a shit," I admitted.

"Ethel can do the fighting for both of you. It's in her blood."

No kidding. "Purple fur."

"Charming and exotic."

Of course she'd think that. She was half elf, and I'd heard enough about elves to be wary. Some said they were crazy. Others claimed they lived to fight.

If Ethel's mother liked my fur, I wasn't going to argue with her. "Beyond that, I don't know."

"Wise, too. Come. I'll show you the library. That's where we'll pinpoint who attacked that guard and dragged you into trouble. Once my baby girl's worked out her nerves, she'll want that settled. Elves don't like threats in their territory."

"Does your library come with an instruction manual on elves?"

Ethel's mother laughed. "Don't run, don't cheat, and expect a diet high in protein. If she starts chewing on you, give her some jerky. That'll give her something to gnaw on."

"Good to know."

WHEN I THOUGHT OF LIBRARIES, books came to mind. I stood in the doorway of a mad scientist's lab blended with a morgue. A few computers, the kind I wished I could afford, were scattered around the room at cluttered workstations. A lone shelf protected with glass held a collection of books I estimated were at least a hundred years old, and unless I'd lost my mind, I was willing to bet they were bound with human skin, likely the victim of someone who'd annoyed one of Ethel's ancestors.

I remembered some of my basic biology courses; unlike most magic species, elves could exist even when there wasn't any magic in the world. Lycanthropes did, too, although it was harder to contract the virus without a source of strong magic.

"All right, sugar. First up is your DNA sample, that way if some other dumbfuck tries to steal you from my baby girl, you'll be easier to track. It'll also give us a chance to check your genetics so we can be ready for your contributions to the family line."

As I wasn't anywhere near brave enough to tell an elf no, I held out my hand so she could steal some of my blood from near my elbow. She stole an entire vial before she was happy. "Before infection, I was mostly vanilla."

"Good. Ethel needs a challenge. How vanilla, sugar? They tell you the percentage?"

"Ninety-seven percent human."

Ethel's mother blinked. "Well I'll be damned. You don't get much purer than that nowadays. What are you now?"

"Ninety-five and a half. I was ninety-six after confirmed infection. I don't think I'll be losing any more genetic points; been a few years since I developed the hybrid form."

"One and a half percentage points of lycanthrope, ninety-five and change human, and three percent of what?"

"The CDC wouldn't tell me."

Ethel's mother giggled and passed the vial to Ethel's uncle. "Alan, be a dear and find out what our little boy here is while I start looking into the idiot who started this mess."

"Welcome to hell, son."

From the little I knew about elves, they were violent, territorial, and took offense to a lot of things, especially those who touched their property—and people counted as property to them. Had I been wise, I would've begun planning my escape the instant I'd learned Ethel was a quarter elf so the rest of her family wouldn't decide I was part of their territory.

Accepting the inevitable would make my life easier. "I'm not leaving here until the culprit's found, am I?"

"No wonder she likes you. You use your head." Ethel's mother flashed me a smile.

Vampires dreamed of having incisors like hers, and a few tigers would get fang envy, too. Why hadn't I found a way to escape? With her teeth, I could easily believe she could eat anything she wanted with little difficulty. "Thank you, ma'am."

"Missy or Mom," she ordered. "Only Ethel gets away with Ma."

Like with Ethel, I couldn't resist testing my luck and her temperament to learn how I'd have to handle the rest of my life. "If I called you Ma and you killed me, would you or Ethel win the resulting fight?"

"I've changed my mind. You can call me your ma if you'd like. I've seen that gleam in my daughter's eyes enough times to know you'll test your luck because you can. Just do me the favor of waiting for when I'm around when you test my baby girl's patience."

Why not? I had nothing to lose, and if Ethel's mother

liked me, she might rescue my ass when I crossed the line too far. "I'll try."

"Smart boy. All right." Ethel's mother rubbed her hands together and sat in front of the nearest workstation, grabbing a sleek laptop beside the large monitor half buried under what I thought was building blueprints. "Start talking, sugar. What do you know about the vic?"

I gave her all the details I knew about Mr. Santiago Jones, his work, and the hybrid wanting to claim him as her mate.

"Well, shit. That's dumber than dumb. He'd be infected soon enough without help. That probably eliminates her pack unless he done told the bitch no, and considering she brought the whole pack out, she was confident in her chances. Any confirmations?"

"An angel verified the hybrid wasn't involved. Unknown about the rest of the pack." I explained my suspicions about Mr. Coolridge and the mall management.

"It's easier to accept a cursed friend than an unknown. Stupid to us, sensible to them—and ignorant all around, since it'll be years for that guard to be of use."

"That was the conclusion we'd come to," I admitted.

"Missy, the attacker was a professional who covered his tracks. We're not finding the lycanthrope. He was too thorough in his cleanup."

"I don't care about the lycanthrope. I care about who hired the lycanthrope—and *I* haven't looked into the matter yet, as my baby girl is a worrywart whiner."

"You're going to get Ethel in trouble with the CDC again."

"Nonsense. If the CDC didn't want me poking my nose in their business, they wouldn't have assigned her to the case. It's not *my* fault the CDC has rules against hiring elves."

"If they have a problem with hiring elves, why'd they hire Ethel?" I asked.

"They're stupid. They think since she's only a quarter she won't eat them. Pussycats, all of them. Ethel's good at what she does, and she doesn't attack without solid provocation. The lycanthropy virus makes them feel better about it."

"But you're infected with lycanthropy," I pointed out. "Wouldn't that make you suitable for CDC hire?"

"I'm also half. Don't worry your pretty head about it, sugar. I'm a card they only play when they're out of options. Anyway, I'm sure they'd love to hire me if they have an army of idiots they need to eliminate."

I worried for the world. "How often do you think the CDC needs someone capable of taking out an entire army?"

"They've thought about it a few times, but they don't like how much I cost."

"Dare I ask?"

"Well, before Ethel picked you, I was going to make them find a suitable partner for her plus a million for a day's worth of work. They thought about it, too. Things worked out without my intervention, so I was only paid fifty grand as my retainer fee."

"Let's say there was someone who really annoyed me or bothered Ethel, how much to make the problem disappear?"

"Lethally or non-lethally?"

I discarded everything I'd believed about the horrors of a relationship with potential in-laws: I had somehow won the lottery of life with the best—albeit craziest—future mother-in-law on the planet. "Both for sake of budgeting purposes."

"If I have to leave them alive, I demand a single grand-puppy. The rest is on the house, as I don't like when people annoy my family."

"I'm formally notifying you I'm a wolf. As such, I'm an opportunist, and any agreements resulting in children will include a stipulation that any in-laws involved will be required to contribute to said child's college fund and upbringing fees."

"You're going to bleed me dry if I give you an inch, aren't you?" Ethel's mother complained. "You're a brave boy."

"Or too stupid to climb out the window calmly to avoid giving the impression of running for my life as I don't want to be eaten by my future mate's mother."

"Near future."

"That's the idea."

"We have strict rules about eating family. An elf only eats a family member if they've broken the code."

"I need an instruction manual."

Ethel's uncle laughed and plopped down in front of one of the lab stations, getting to work testing my DNA to get a genetics report. "We all do, son."

"I don't get why you aren't afraid. *Everyone* who isn't an elf—" Ethel's mother blinked. "Alan? Test to see if any of those unknown genes include elf."

"That's what I was thinking, Missy. If he has a dominant gene in his unknown percentages, he wouldn't be afraid of you or even your ma."

"How long will it take to run?"

"Don't get your panties in a bunch, Missy. Not long, especially if I do a confirmation scan rather than a full diagnostic."

"Why do you have so much equipment in here anyway?" I asked.

Ethel's mother laughed. "We're who the CDC go to when

they have a mystery even they can't solve. I also run a little lab for those who want information without nosy law enforcement knowing about it. Elves are excellent at that line of work. We can tell when bones have been chewed on, hacked apart—you have a mystery dealing with bones, and without fail, we can figure out the truth. Even from a fragment."

If I read between the lines, not difficult to do with so much evidence around me, I'd landed head first into a legal mess. Had I cared more about the law, I might've been disturbed by my conclusions. "Okay, I'm impressed. You're part of the black market the CDC can't access?"

"She brought me home a smart one, Alan. I'm so proud."

"One and a half percent elf, Missy."

"What's the other one and a half percent?"

"Going to have to run a scan. It'll be a few minutes."

"This explains so much. Of course she'd find herself an elf."

"One and a half percent hardly classifies me as an elf," I muttered.

"Alan? Why did my baby girl have to pick a fearless elf male?"

"She cries when her crushes run away, Miss. We've talked about this before. And no, you can't bite him—or her former crushes for running away."

"They should be groveling at her feet!"

"While this is true, remember how frustrating it was when my brother kept running away? How long did it take you to convince him you weren't going to murder him in his sleep following conception?"

Some stories were worth hearing, and I held my breath hoping they'd continue the discussion and offer more insights into the wondrous horrors that was the Frankwell family.

"That's my mother's fault for using my father's skull as a purse! I didn't do anything, damn it."

My mouth dropped open. "She used his skull as a purse? But why?"

Ethel's uncle laughed. "Remember this when he does something you don't like, Missy. He asked why."

"Humans. My father died of old age, boy. My mother missed him. It's elven custom. She wore his skull on her hip for ten years—the customary time of grieving. Now she shows him off to frighten the humans."

No wonder they ate those who cheated; if Ethel's mother was to be believed, partnerships were serious business to them. Ten years of mourning would make most people seem excessive. "That's oddly sweet," I admitted. "She must have loved him a lot."

Ethel's mother smiled, and something about her eyes softened, full of the sort of melancholy for a lost love so deep it could never be erased. "She did. He was loyal, and there's little else more important to an elf than loyalty."

"Like lycanthropes."

"Essentially."

Ethel's uncle burst into laughter. "Ethel's done landed herself an interesting one, Missy."

"What'd you find?"

"I figured I'd check the exotics databases on genetics first to eliminate the data crunching the machine had to do, and it didn't take long to get a hit on that last percentage."

"Seriously, I thought it took hours to crunch out this information," I muttered. "Days, even."

"Quiet, son. I ain't talkin' to you."

"But those are my genes."

"Quiet, son."

I sighed.

"Stop playing around, Alan. What is he?"

"It looks like Sjöfn had a dalliance with one of the ljósálfar seven or so generations ago. Maybe six. Six generations would be roughly a percent and a half."

"Norse? He's Norse?" Ethel's mother wailed. "That's not fair. My line is of Celtic origin."

"Don't worry about her whining, son. She's just jealous because the ljósálfar were few and far between. Celts were more likely to roam, and don't get her started about the Asiatic elves; they outnumber the Celtic elves five to one."

"How many of these..." I couldn't pronounce the name he'd given to the variant of elf I supposedly was.

"Not many, at least not on Earth. They play by divine rules, so they don't visit often. Celtic and Asiatic elves stay on Earth and have no divine aspirations."

"Who the hell would want to rule over the heavens anyway? Boring!" Ethel's mother declared.

"So, that explains a lot. That three percent pre-infection is why he is as he is. When your great-great-great-great-grandmother is a goddess of love and your great-great-great-great-grandfather is an elf, you're going to be serious about your partner. Add in some lycanthropy and otherwise pure human, and you're going to be loyal to a fault, interested in only one person at a time, and eternally patient since elves and the divine have shitty conceptions of time."

"Alan, your job is to play with his genetics and extend his longevity."

"No, Missy. We are not experimenting with his genetics."

"Yes, we are."

"No, we aren't."

"Yes, we are."

Ethel's uncle drew in a deep breath and bellowed, "Ethel! Your ma is planning her grandchildren. Rescue your male before she makes me adjust his DNA for breeding purposes!"

"I didn't say that, you idiot. I said make him live longer, not breed more efficiently."

"That would be next."

Ethel's mother scowled. "True."

"Next, you'll be giving him those aphrodisiac-laced candies you made me make when you heard your baby girl had found a man."

"Aphrodisiac candy?" I blurted.

Ethel's mother reached into her pocket and pulled out a handful of pink candies in clear wrappers. "These. Four for you, two for her, and I promise you'll have the night of your life."

Ethel came barreling into the lab, skidded to a halt, and snarled, "You will *not* do genetic experiments on Dale!"

I wasn't sure which worried me more: Ethel's confidence her family would attempt to modify my DNA or my acceptance of the insanity.

I reached out and counted out six of the candies. "Thank you."

"Don't take anything from her. It's a trap. She could be sedating you, she could be giving you an illegal substance, *you never know with her*. Don't do it!"

"Aphrodisiac-laced candies, four for me, two for you," I replied, careful to keep my expression neutral while staring her in the eyes. "I've been promised we'll have the night of our lives."

"Oh." Ethel blinked. "Oh."

"I think she likes me."

Ethel's mother laughed. "I wouldn't give your Dale any illegal substances. However, I do demand you marry this man immediately."

"Ma!"

"Go on and take Dale to your room, have some candy, enjoy yourself. I'll have your father bring you something for dinner and leave it in the hall. You didn't kill him this time, did you?"

"Tossed his lazy ass in the pool. He didn't drown because I have stupid, interfering sisters."

"What about your brothers?"

"Chicken shits."

Ethel's mother rolled her eyes. "Go claim your man. I'll go tame the rest of the family. Try not to break the house too much, please. Come along, Alan. Let's leave the lovebirds alone."

"Do *not* trash the lab," Ethel's uncle ordered, glaring at us both.

I waited for them to leave before I held out my hand to Ethel and smiled. "Shall we?"

Her smile was the only answer I needed.

No Kitten Around is the next book in the Magical Romantic Comedy (with a body count) series. These stories, with the exception of Burn, Baby, Burn (sequel to Playing with Fire,) can be read in any order.

Afterword

Like with Serial Killer Princess, this is the story of how two people joined forces. Under threat of maiming from the editor, Dale and Ethel's story will continue.

And yes, you'll find out who went after that poor security guard and why, what the deal was with that bat-winged blight, and other little tidbits the author has greedily kept to herself so she can have excuses to write about Missy.

RJ Blain and the Finned and Furred Management hope you have enjoyed this novella, which is intended to be a fun escape from life for a while.

Sometimes, even the author needs to step away and just have some fun every now and then, and this novella was that fun.

The continuation of this novella will continue in a future Magical Romantic Comedy (with a body count) anthology. Release date TBD.

About R.J. Blain

RJ BLAIN suffers from a Moleskine journal obsession, a pen fixation, and a terrible tendency to pun without warning.

When she isn't playing pretend, she likes to think she's a cartographer and a sumi-e painter.

In her spare time, she daydreams about being a spy. Should that fail, her contingency plan involves tying her best of enemies to spinning wheels and quoting James Bond villains until she is satisfied.

RJ also writes as Susan Copperfield, Bernadette Franklin, Audrey Greene, G.P. Robbins, and Lilith Daniels. Visit RJ and her pets (the Management) at thesneakykittycritic.com.

FOLLOW RJ & HER ALTER EGOS ON BOOKBUB:
RJ BLAIN
SUSAN COPPERFIELD
BERNADETTE FRANKLIN
G.P. ROBBINS

Audrey Greene
Lilith Daniels